KEEPING CAROLINE

Survivor & Savior Duet Book 2

C.A. VARIAN

Book Cover by Leigh Cover Designs

Editing by Willow Oaks Author Services & Wiski Publishing, LLC.

Internal formatting by me

Art by Swampy Sloth Studios and Wallflower Designs

Printed Edges by Painted Wings Publishing

1st edition 2024

To Trina
♡ CaVara

For anyone who feels like the grief is too much or life is just too f*CKING hard. You ARE stronger than you think. You are loved, wanted, and needed here. Don't give up the FIGHT.
This book is for you.

CaVarian

We miss and love you, Shawn

for Jerime.

Leukemia took you
from us way too
young, at only seven
years old, and we've
missed you ever since.

Love you forever,
Pie Wie.

Trigger Warnings

There are many mature themes throughout Keeping Caroline. It is not intended for readers under 17 years of age.

The following themes are explored in this book and are not limited to: graphic (consensual) sexual content, graphic violence, abduction, graphic descriptions of aberrant violence and torture, vulgar language, suicide ideation, loss of a spouse, sick child, and murder.

Prologue

The Phoenix

Pushing a chair against the door and wedging its back under the doorknob, I let out a shaky breath and desperately reached for my phone. I was not sure why my instincts led my fingers to pull up the contact info for someone I had only spoken to a few times. Although he had been working with my brother for a long time, I had only met him when he came into the store, but he was someone I knew could help me—or at least I hoped he could.

Swallowing back my hesitation, I clicked on his contact information and quickly typed a message. "Hey, it's Caroline. I think I need your help."

CHAPTER 1

The Phoenix

Two Weeks Earlier

It's startling how fast life can change—how quickly you can go from whole to a million broken fragments, tumbling along the ground and breaking into dust. That's what happened to me three years ago when my husband, Daniel, died in a car crash, leaving me and Evie, our then five-year-old daughter, to navigate life without him. After three years of being without him, I was not sure if I would ever be able to move on.

Dawn cast a gentle glow across the small cottage kitchen as I stared out the window, but even as sunshine painted my face with its joyous rays, he was all I could think about. I did not believe in an afterlife, but I couldn't help but wonder if he was watching over us—if he knew how hard his little girl fought against cancer—how hard she had *been* fighting. Evie had been in remission for five months, but I wondered every day if the cancer was back and hiding from us. It haunted me like a bomb with a retractable fuse, except I wasn't the one holding the lighter. I couldn't even find the fuse.

Our new home in the mountains of Alabama was so different from my downtown New Orleans apartment, but I loved it. It was the perfect place to raise my little girl. It was far away from the hustle and bustle of a city that moved too fast, a city that was plagued with too much crime and natural disasters that sent us running multiple times per year like birds flying away from the seasons that did not suit them.

I moved quietly, trying not to wake Evelyn, acutely aware of the peaceful stillness that enveloped the house without the incessant horns of taxis outside our windows. I cracked eggs into the sizzling pan, the aroma of butter and bacon filling the air, making my stomach grumble. It definitely beat the hospital food that had all started to taste like cardboard after a while. The steady rhythm of my morning routine provided a comforting anchor in a world that had once been untethered by grief.

"Mommy?" A sleepy voice drifted in from the hallway, pulling a smile onto my lips. After so many months of not having my little girl at home, I cherished every moment we had together. Just thinking about how I could have lost her forever threatened to send me into a downward spiral that I would never crawl out of, so I pushed the what-ifs away, instead focusing on making every moment with her as special as I could. Cancer was a relentless foe, but Evie was a warrior.

"Good morning, nugget." Turning off the burner, I watched as Evelyn appeared around the corner, the stuffed llama Ethan had brought her the last time she was in the Intensive Care Unit clutched tightly in her arms. She padded over to the table, dragging her feet in fluffy bunny slippers.

As she sat down, I measured out her medications, a morning routine we had perfected over countless months.

"It tastes yucky, Mommy." Watching me with her usual scowl, Evie shook her head. She responded the same way every day, but we both knew she would take her medicine in the end. She had no other choice if she was going to stay in remission.

I smiled, setting the bottle back on the counter. "Like the nastiest goblin brew, but it's making you strong, my little warrior."

Her blue eyes searched mine, seeking assurance in a world upended too soon. "Strong like you?"

The question took me by surprise, considering I was never more than two seconds from unraveling. "Stronger."

Once she had bravely downed her medicine and taken a big gulp of her vanilla almond milk to wash it down, I returned to the stove to finish making breakfast. My heart swelled with love as I prepared her food on her favorite plate, ensuring every detail was perfect—the strawberries sliced in bite-sized pieces so she would not choke, and her toast buttered just how she liked it.

"Here you go, baby. Eat up. We've got a big day ahead."

As she nibbled, I fitted her hairpiece on her still nearly bald head, pulling the sides back in a braid and finishing it in a big pink bow.

"Is Uncle Ethan coming for breakfast too?" she asked, a milk mustache coloring the top of her lip.

Right on cue, the sound of a familiar engine rumbled outside, and moments later my brother sauntered in, his black hair disheveled and tattoos peeking out from his rolled-up sleeves. With late spring setting in, it was getting too hot for his typical black hoodie, not that he didn't still wear it the majority of the time.

"Morning, Cara. Morning, munchkin." A goofy grin spread across his lips as he crossed the room and lifted Evie from her chair, her squeal nearly popping my eardrums. She thrashed, but it only made him tickle her harder, her wig barely holding on.

"Put me down, silly goose!"

Chuckling, he plopped her back into her chair and sat beside her.

"Saved you some eggs and bacon," I said, sliding a plate across the table, followed by a mug of black coffee. It felt like a ritual, this shared meal we had most mornings, a silent nod to the new life we were steadily building in Alabama, far from the turmoil that once consumed us. "Is Scarlett at the store?"

Already chewing his food, he nodded, the love for his new wife written all over his face. There was still so much I didn't know about how they'd met, but what I did know was that their love was one I hoped for myself one day. It was a force that could build and shatter worlds—just like I'd had with Daniel, turning my whole world upside down.

Thoughts of the man I still mourned flooded my mind again, tearing at the freshly stitched wound that still bled, so I did my best to push it back. Later. Later, when I was alone, I would let myself feel.

"Are you excited for school?" Ethan asked, his bright blue eyes settling on Evie, whose fingers were so sticky that I instinctively clenched my teeth, hoping she wouldn't get any in her new wig.

"Uh-huh," she mumbled between bites of her fruit, nodding enthusiastically.

"Good. You're going to knock 'em dead today." Taking another sip of his coffee, he returned his eyes to me. "You settling in okay at the bookstore? You seem to like it."

"Better than okay." I smiled, the thought of Tangled in the Pages Two, the bookstore he and Scarlett had just opened, sending warmth straight into my heart. "It's like finding a piece of myself I thought I'd lost."

Ethan nodded, understanding without needing further explanation. We'd both sacrificed pieces of ourselves along the way—his to the darkness, mine to despair. Yet here we were, piecing them back together, side by side, the only family we had left.

"Scarlett's lucky to have you," he said after a moment, his tone laced with pride.

It was amazing to see my brother settling down and smiling. His happiness and love showed in everything he did, in every glance toward Scarlett. She was his world. I couldn't imagine ever dating again, not after losing the love of my life, but if I ever did, I hoped to have what they did. Theirs was the kind of love that filled your chest until there was no room for hurt; the kind of love that left you breathless.

Reaching across the table, I wrapped my hand around his, needing my brother to know how important he was to me. "And I'm lucky to have her... and you. Maybe one day, I'll find something like what the two of you have, but I have a feeling it's a once in a lifetime thing, and I've already had my soulmate."

Pulling into the drop off lane, I squeezed Evie's hand, the ritual as much a comfort to me as it was to her. She was only on a hybrid school schedule, going to school three days per week, but having her away from me was hard. I'd only just gotten her back. "Remember, I'll pick you up right after school."

"I know, Mommy." Her smile was the kind that crinkled her nose and made her entire face glow. "And then we can go to the bookstore and see Auntie Scarlett!"

"We can certainly do that, nugget." The familiar tug at my heartstrings sent a smile onto my face as well. Letting go was never easy, but this routine—our little morning dance of reassurances—had become the steady beat to the start of each day, whether she was going to school or not.

With a quick kiss on my cheek, she pulled on her backpack, the one adorned with vibrant stickers she'd chosen herself, and joined the crowd of children bustling through the school doors. I lingered for a moment longer, ensuring she melded safely into the sea of uniforms before I finally drove away.

The drive to Tangled in the Pages Two was short, only three miles from Evie's school. As I parked and stepped out onto the sidewalk, the late spring air filled my lungs, carrying with it the scent of freshly brewed coffee mixing with the fresh mountain air, nothing like what we had lived with in New Orleans.

The bells above the door chimed as I walked in and my gaze immediately found Ethan, who was lifting a box of newly arrived books onto the counter. Customers milled about, their fingers trailing over spines, while a few stood at the cafe counter.

"Need a hand?" I asked him, slipping behind the counter and grabbing my apron.

A smile spread across my brother's lips, one I was seeing increasingly as of late. "I've got it, Cara, but we may need some help at the register."

I nodded, aiming for the front of the store. "Got it."

Heading toward the register, I passed Scarlett as she meticulously arranged a display of books, unconsciously stopping to rub her baby bump. It was a testament to the new life they were building together and how far she had come since her ex-husband, Joshua—who was thankfully no longer wasting oxygen—had tried to erase her existence. When she noticed me, she smiled, her dark eyes lighting up with genuine affection. "Good morning, Caroline."

With a few customers at the register and only one cashier handling everyone, I didn't stop to chat, but I touched her forearm as I passed. "Good morning. That looks great."

Even in a small mountain town, there was a steady stream of customers throughout the day, making time go by quickly. Between helping customers, restocking shelves, and brewing cups of coffee for those seeking a quiet corner to immerse themselves in a good book, I ran around all day, barely finding time to take a break. If anything, it prevented me from getting lost in my head, a place I sometimes needed an escape from.

Arriving back at the bookstore with Evie in tow later that afternoon, I'd barely put the car in park before she jumped out of the car and bolted into the building. After a long day at school, I would have thought she would have had less energy. I was exhausted.

Crouching, Scarlett wrapped Evie in a hug. "Hey, sweetie! How was your day?"

Before Evie had a chance to answer, Ethan grabbed her and lifted her off the ground, tickling her sides and sending her into a fit of giggles. "We got a new toy train today, munchkin. Wanna play with it?"

"Y-y-yes. P-p-put me down!"

CHAPTER 2
The Phantom

The glow of multiple screens was the only light in the room, emitting an eerie luminescence over the scattered hardware and half-empty coffee cups and soda cans that seemed to accumulate on every surface in my computer room. My downtown apartment was large, but my lab was where I spent the majority of my time. With the number of clients who called on my services regularly, I was never away from a device for long. Aside from my clients, who I rarely met face to face, my cat, Houdini, and Legacy, my mentor and the man who got me off the streets, I kept to myself.

Sitting in front of my center monitor, my fingers danced across the keyboard, a rhythmic melody to the uninitiated, to those unfamiliar with the world of computer hacking, but to me, each keystroke was a familiar symphony of code. The digital fortress I had constructed around myself in my home was more than just a workspace. It was a haven—a retreat from a world that demanded too much connection, too much emotion. Having lost my parents at sixteen, I had always found it safer to stay firmly within my bubble, my only roots being the wires that connected my technology to its power source.

"Phantom" was not just a moniker. It was my reality. In my lab, amidst the hum of the machines and the flicker of lines rushing past across monitors, I could disappear. It was a somber existence punctuated by the crackle of electrical circuits and the occasional purr of my furry companion, who seemed to appreciate the quiet as much as I did. He was good company, so I wasn't truly alone.

A soft ping broke the silence, a simple notification sound, yet it sent a ripple through the stillness of my sanctum. It was Ethan—Bane—or Boss, as I usually called him. The encrypted message came across my device, finding me in my self-imposed exile.

"Need you at the new cabin in AL. Security setup. Can you make the trip?"

I paused, feeling the weight of the outside world pressing against the walls of my apartment. Ethan didn't ask for favors often. The man was a fortress himself, all hard edges, inked skin, and haunted eyes that had seen too much. Yet there was honor in him, and a protectiveness that extended beyond his immediate circle, but getting too close to him could put me in the line of fire, and I knew that. Still, after everything we'd uncovered together, I couldn't find it in myself to turn him down.

"Sure," I typed back, my fingers pausing before pressing send. "When?"

Three pulsing dots. Tapping my finger on my mouse, I took a sip of my soda, knowing I should probably switch to water if I wanted to sleep at some point before daylight. "Tomorrow good?"

"See you then." My response was automatic, but as I leaned back in my chair, staring into the light of my computer screens, responsibility and a warning warred inside my chest. Ethan and Scarlett's world was one of dark pasts and tangled futures. Although this time it was pulling me to rural Alabama, to where they'd recently moved and opened a bookstore, it was so much more than their attempt to start over with used novels and dog-eared paperbacks. They may have moved there to leave their past behind, but I wasn't so sure if the past was through with them yet. The question was, if their past wasn't finished with them, did I want to risk it catching up with my present?

Sleek black fur blending in with the shadows, Houdini jumped onto the desk, his bright emerald eyes reflecting the screens' lights like beacons. As he nuzzled my hand, forcing me to give him attention, it was a not-so-subtle reminder that even in the depths of my isolation, connections were inevitable, maybe even necessary.

Sliding behind the wheel of my vintage, black, 1969 Mustang, the engine rumbled to life with a roar that echoed off the walls of the parking garage below my apartment complex. As I pulled out onto the freeway, I watched the city fade into the rearview mirror, a tangle of glass and steel vanishing into the horizon behind me.

Breathing in deeply, my lungs filled with the scent of the fresh air blowing in through the open windows, it was a stark contrast to the car exhaust I was used to. Urban chaos slowly bled into pastoral calm as I drove. Skyscrapers gave way to sprawling fields and the constant hum of traffic softened to the occasional murmur of passing cars. The golden rays of the sun glinted off the hood as I steered the car along the highway, cutting through rural Georgia. Rolling hills stretched as far as the eye could see, dotted with grazing horses and weathered barns.

But even with the serene landscape outside my windows, however, with every mile, the anticipation within me swelled, a silent storm that thrummed against my ribcage. I wasn't naive. I knew the risk I could be taking by meeting Ethan and Scarlett face to face—how their enemies, the remaining members of Victor Delacroix's gang that were undoubtedly still out there, could finally realize I was the man behind the screens and seek vengeance against me for the part I'd played in their leader's death—the part I was still playing. I may not have been the one who'd pulled the trigger when Ethan stormed into one of their locations to save Scarlett and killed several people in the process, including their leader, but I'd helped him find them, and I'd helped to create the diversions that had gotten him inside, and them both back out. But after everything we'd gone through together, I considered them my friends, so I swallowed my hesitation down like the jagged pill it was, and pressed my foot harder against the pedal, loving the way my baby purred beneath me. Damn, I loved my car.

Living in Atlanta, I didn't make my way to this part of Alabama often. My job required me to remain in locations with high-speed internet at least, and by the lack of infra-structure as I approached the eastern border of Alabama, I realized I may be out of luck. The Appalachian Mountains stood sentinel in the distance, the sun illuminating their peaks like golden crowns. It was breathtaking—a contrast to the constant flashing of police lights and the sterile chill of skyscrapers.

It was still early in the morning by the time I exited off the freeway toward the town where Ethan and Scarlett lived, venturing deeper into the mountains. Wanting to avoid rush hour traffic, I'd left way too early, so I was relieved when the illuminated sign for my hotel popped up around the bend. Ethan wasn't expecting me until later in the day, and I needed a nap. After his message, I'd stayed awake for far too long packing, and dwelling on if I was making the right decision. No matter what argument I made with myself, however, I'd still decided to take the risk. I hoped I didn't come to regret it.

The small town where Ethan and Scarlett opened their new bookstore in was quaint, a place you would see in a romance holiday movie, a town where everyone in town came out just to watch the Christmas tree being lit on Main Street. There was a charm to this town that I would never be able to find in the place I called home, and I could certainly see the appeal.

Pulling my backpack on, I left the hotel and stepped out into the early spring afternoon, heading down the street toward Tangled in the Pages Two, which was only two blocks away.

The scent of pine filled the air as I pulled in a deep breath and scanned the quiet street. It was not quite time for schools to let out, but I imagined the roads and sidewalks became busier once they did.

My steps became less sure as the bookstore came into view, but I forged forward, stepping through the door just as another man walked out, allowing me to walk in unnoticed.

For a moment, I lingered near the stack of bestsellers at the entrance, taking everything in. Although I'd never seen pictures of Ethan, I'd seen many of Scarlett, so I recognized her immediately. Petite, with long black hair and deep brown eyes, Scarlett was a stunning woman, and the way her eyes lit up as she smiled at her husband, her hand reaching down to rub the small swell of her pregnant stomach, even my icy heart warmed for her. Out of everyone in the world, she deserved so much happiness. And Ethan, at least in person, at least in such a benign setting, had far fewer shadows than I ever expected him to have. They seemed almost...*ordinary*.

A smile stretching across my lips, I stepped away from the place where I'd been lingering, moving closer to the counter. "Hey, Boss. I heard this was the place to get a good cup of coffee in town."

Both Ethan and Scarlett spun toward me, Ethan's eyes widening, amusement playing across his features although he was the one who'd invited me. "Phantom?"

"Nice to finally meet you," I said, extending a hand toward Ethan before turning my smile toward Scarlett, who'd moved to stand by his side. "And this must be Scarlett."

A bright smile spread across her lips, and before I knew what was happening, she took a step forward and pulled me into a hug. "Hello. It's amazing to finally meet you!"

Although it was awkward, and she'd nearly knocked my glasses off my face, I hugged her back. "It's nice to meet you too."

As she pulled away, I noticed the stunning woman and little girl standing near the cafe counter—a woman who looked remarkably like Ethan, so I assumed she was his sister. Seeming to sense my eyes on her, she turned up to look at me, the side of her lips lifting in a smile. Before I could lift my hand in a wave, she turned and chased after her little girl who'd taken off in the other direction, running toward the back of the store.

It was impossible not to chuckle, but I redirected my attention back to Scarlett and Ethan. "I heard the two of you may be in need of a new security system, and I definitely wanted to come check out the new store. By the way, my real name is Tristan."

I'd debated the entire way to the store whether I wanted to share my real name with them, but since I knew their names, I figured it was only fair they knew mine. The three of us had moved past simple acquaintances. If Ethan trusted me with his family's safety, then I needed to trust him with mine.

Ethan smiled, reaching forward to grip my forearm. "Appreciate you making the trip, Tristan."

Nodding, I flicked my eyes over his shoulder to where the other woman had reappeared from around the stacks, her bright blue eyes meeting mine before turning away.

"Tristan, that over there is my sister, Caroline," Ethan said, letting go of my arm to lift the little girl who'd wrapped her arms around his leg and was hanging off him like a monkey. "And this little firecracker is Evie."

Caroline smiled at me, her beauty nearly sending me to my knees, but it was her little girl that tugged at my heart.

Although I didn't know much about Ethan's family, it was clear by the child's appearance that she was a cancer patient, which was heartbreaking for someone so young, but when she looked up at me, it was also clear she was bursting with life.

"Hi, Tristan!" Her voice was bright as a string of lights, her eyes wide and curious. "Are you a superhero? You look like someone who knows about secret missions!"

A chuckle escaped me, despite the somberness that often lay beneath my smiles. "Not exactly a superhero, Evie. But I do know a thing or two about secret missions." I winked, watching as her grin widened, revealing a gap where a tooth had vacated its post.

The way Ethan held Evie in his arms, it was easy to forget how much blood he'd spilled. "Tristan's going to help us with top secret computer stuff," he said, his tone making me sound so much cooler than I really was. Giving her a kiss on the cheek, he placed her back on the ground.

"Like in spy movies?" she asked, bouncing on the balls of her feet. I had to admit, she was an adorable kid.

Loving the lightness that bubbled inside me at her exuberance, I grinned. "Exactly like a spy movie."

The air was crisp, carrying with it the scent of the forest after it rained. I followed behind Ethan and Scarlett as they walked hand-in-hand through the grass of their expansive property. Up ahead of us, Evie skipped with a stuffed llama in her arms, powered by a seemingly endless supply of energy. Beside me, Caroline walked quietly, the floral scent of her shampoo nearly sending my eyes rolling back in my head. I couldn't imagine what Ethan would say if he knew I was already crushing on his sister, and to be honest, I wasn't sure if I cared.

Although I didn't know anything about Ethan's finances, I was privy to what Scarlett had received after her husband's death, as well what she'd received when her trust fund was finally released by her father, and it was clear some of it had gone into the property we toured while the heat of the day cooled. She'd brought quite a bit of wealth into her marriage with Ethan.

Tucked within the towering pines, the sizable wooden structure seemed to be part of the forest—beautiful in its simplicity. Aside from the cabin, there were three other structures on the property, including a barn, all of which blended into the landscape.

"Big place," I said, gazing out at the sun as it made its way behind the endless peaks. "It's really peaceful. How many acres do you have here?"

Ethan smiled, letting go of Scarlett's hand so he could wrap his arm around her waist and pull her close. There was no question as to how much they loved each other. It only served to make me feel lonelier—an awareness that always seemed to cut deeper when you were around others than when you were truly alone. For a moment, I wondered what Caroline's story was—what had happened to Evie's father—but it wasn't my business, so I had no intention of asking.

"In total, about forty acres," Ethan responded, pointing toward the distant ridge, where the setting sun painted the sky in a prism of pastels. "But protected forests border us on the other side of that ridge for thousands of square acres, so it gives us a lot of added privacy."

I nodded, appreciating the seclusion for what it was worth but knowing it could never be for me. All I kept thinking was about the lack of cellular signal I'd had ever since we'd arrived at their property. With all the trees, and being so far from town, getting any kind of reliable signal was a challenge.

"It's a lot to secure." Although we both knew it, my words still came out. The grounds were getting dark, but there was already a fire burning in the backyard that he'd started before we'd left for our walk. Scarlett's chin dipped in a nod, but it was Ethan who answered as he turned left on the path, leading us back toward their home.

"It will be, and I hope it's not necessary, but after everything my wife has already been through, I'll do whatever it takes to keep her safe."

As we approached the large back porch of the cabin, Scarlett kissed Ethan on the cheek and let go of his hand, heading into the house, Evie, and Caroline at her heels. Instead of following the others inside, Ethan approached the large outdoor grill, glancing at me before lighting the burner.

"New Orleans is heating up," he said, his eyes flicking up to meet mine before glancing toward the back door. "Victor Delacroix's gang isn't going to lie low forever. You know the FBI's poking around, and if they connect the dots back to Scarlett or her father..." His words trailed off, but the unspoken threat hung in the air, dense and foreboding. I could almost hear the click of a hammer being pulled back, ready to unleash chaos. "If he discovers this haven, if something hap—"

"I won't let them find out." Despite the storm starting to brew inside me, and although we both knew it wasn't a promise I could make, I still meant the words with every fiber of my being. If it was in my power to lead Victor's gang astray, I would. "I'll fortify this place... make it invisible to anyone who doesn't know where to look."

"Appreciate it, man." Ethan's nod was filled with gratitude and the knowledge that the line between protector and predator was one he had walked many times. "Scarlett's got enough to worry about with the baby on the way. She doesn't need the sins of my past—or her father's—to come knocking on our door."

CHAPTER 3
The Phantom

T he evening air held a chill in the mountains that we never got in the concrete jungle I called home. I stood beside Ethan at the grill as he flipped steaks on an open flame, breathing in the fresh scent of nature that mingled with the aroma of seared meat.

"After killing Victor Delacroix... there's no turning back now," Ethan muttered, his light blue eyes reflecting the fire's glow. "His mob won't take it lightly. I didn't have a choice, but they'll want revenge."

I nodded, his words sending a shiver through my body that had nothing to do with the temperature outside. "Even with the FBI potentially watching, you think his people will retaliate?"

"Retaliation is a given," he replied, his gaze fixed on the darkness beyond the halo of light surrounding us from the bonfire and porch lights. "But it's not just them. I don't want Scarlett getting dragged into this thing. There shouldn't have been any evidence left of her in the torched scene, but I'm hoping the feds don't come sniffing around."

The mention of the feds stirred a different kind of unease within me. My mind instinctively began to race, considering all the angles, all the potential digital trails that could lead to an unwanted knock on the door. "How hot do you reckon the trial is? I mean, I haven't seen much on the news yet. Seems like they're keeping it all close to the vest right now."

Ethan exhaled slowly, the tension in his shoulders becoming more pronounced. "Although Scarlett has no contact with her father, we do know they've been digging. Victor's operation was vast—drugs, weapons, you name it. And after what went down with Scarlett's father..." He trailed off, the unsaid words hanging heavy between us.

"Well, I'll do my best to make sure there's no electronic trail of Scarlett being involved, and as far as the remaining members of Victor's gang, all we can do is try to find out if they know who you are, and if they know what Victor had planned for her. There's always the chance that his plans were kept to a small following." Hesitating for a moment, I glanced toward the cabin only yards away, where I could just barely see Scarlett and Caroline through the window as they moved around the kitchen. "This isn't the same location the two of you ran to last time, and everyone who was at that compound... They're—"

"Dead," he cut in. After everything he and Scarlett went through—after everything I was a part of—I understood all that he'd had to do in order to save the woman he loved, but I did not think I could ever get over the idea of taking a life, or if I could ever do such a thing myself.

I nodded, meeting his stare. "Right. They're all dead. So, there is a chance the rest of his gang has no idea that you and Scarlett were involved."

Turning back toward the grill, Ethan flipped the steaks, the sizzling steam making my stomach grumble. "I think there's a higher probability they at least know Scarlett's father was involved, and perhaps may, once again, try to use her to get to her father. But," he said, using the tongs to point to a pan which I held out for him to place the meat on, "we have been doing everything we can to cover our tracks—especially Scarlett's tracks, including changing her name and purchasing the store and home under a different entity altogether. Unless they come here and run into her in the street, they shouldn't be able to easily find her, but that doesn't mean they won't. We just must stay vigilant and be prepared."

With the food cooked, the conversation about Victor Delacroix and the events that had happened in New Orleans ceased. I followed Ethan back inside and we sat down at the long, wooden table where Scarlett, Evie, and Caroline were already seated. The atmosphere was warm and inviting, the cabin itself a true home. It was such a contrast to eating in my dark computer lab from take-out containers. Although I had the ability to toss ingredients together and have them taste half-decent, I didn't cook often. Nobody enjoyed cooking for one. Back when I had a girlfriend... Well, it had been a while. *Two long years*.

"So, what do you think of our little town so far?" Scarlett asked, passing me a dish of steamed vegetables.

"It's beautiful here," I said honestly, my eyes flicking to Caroline's for a moment, surprised when her cheeks flushed a rosy shade. "The scenery is breathtaking, and the people seem genuinely kind."

"Most of them are," Ethan chimed in. "But every town has its fair share of nosy busybodies. We've had to learn how to navigate around them."

His words made me chuckle, and for the life of me, I couldn't help but imagine Ethan, in all his darkness, trying to manage a nosy old lady and keep her in her place. He may have been intimidating, but I think even he would cower to an Alabama mountain grandma with a glass of sweet tea and the words 'bless your heart' on her lips. "Well, it doesn't look like you have any neighbors near the cabin at least."

The look on Ethan's face told me it had very much been the plan. I didn't blame him. Although I liked living where modern conveniences were a dime a dozen, I preferred to not hear my neighbors fucking through the walls. "Did you see the fight last night?" he asked, a casualness in his tone that didn't quite reach his eyes. "That knockout was brutal."

"Missed it," I admitted, taking a sip of my beer. "Was running diagnostics on my systems."

Scarlett laughed softly from her seat beside Ethan. "You and your computers. Sometimes I wonder if you dream in code."

"Doesn't everyone?" I didn't miss how Caroline's lips lifted in a smile at my response, which stirred something low in my belly. Beside her, Evie had ketchup all over her face, but seemed to be the happiest kid on the planet, no matter what was brewing beneath the surface of her skin. It was something I still hadn't asked about.

Dinner unfolded with an ease that surprised me. We talked about the weather, the clarity of the night sky so far up in the mountains, and the latest book Scarlett was reading. I listened more than I spoke, letting the voices fill the spaces between us. It was strange, this budding sense of camaraderie between Ethan and I, two men who lived in the shadows now breaking bread under the same roof. It was odd, but I realized the longer I was in their company, the more I was open to it.

"Super-spy Tristan," Evie's small voice interrupted, her bright blue eyes fixed on me from where she sat across the table. She stood, clutching a stuffed llama in her arms, its fur matted from countless hugs.

"Hey, sweetheart." Pushing my chair back, I leaned forward to lower myself to her level. "What's up?"

She twisted on her feet, as though she was nervous to say whatever she wanted to say. "Will you play with me?"

"Of course," I replied without hesitation. "Lead the way, Captain."

Her laughter was like music as she took my hand and pulled me toward the bedroom Ethan and Scarlett had set up for her in their home. The walls were adorned with drawings, her imagination splashed across every inch. Leading me across the room to a shelf that was lined with action figures, she told me all about them, each with their own intricate backstory, and I found myself engrossed, following her narratives with genuine interest. I hadn't been a child in a long time, but I admittedly missed the imagination that tended to fade with adulthood. I was still only twenty-six, but trauma had certainly already turned my life to gray.

As we built a castle out of her Legos and devised an epic tale of how her queen saved the entire kingdom from all the bad guys, I let the weight of the world slide from my shoulders—if only for a little while.

The laughter from Evie's room faded into a gentle hum of a lullaby as Caroline's voice threaded through the crack under the door. They weren't staying for the night, but Scarlett and Caroline wanted to watch a movie together while Ethan and I worked, and Evie couldn't keep her eyes open, so Caroline bathed and put her to bed before it began. I stood in the hallway for a moment, a little out of place as to where to go next. I'd ridden to the cabin with Ethan, therefore I didn't have a vehicle to get myself back to the hotel. I wasn't sure who intended to deposit me back in town, but I knew someone would at some point.

"Tristan," Ethan said, coming around the corner from the living area, nearly startling me half to death. "Ready to see the brains of the operation?"

The corner of my mouth lifted as I nodded. "Hell, yes. I've been waiting to see some tech."

With the women still in the living area and the scent of popcorn meeting my nose, I followed Ethan down the main hallway and into a spacious master suite. A massive bed made of carved dark wood stood in the center of the main wall, with complimenting pieces of furniture spread out in the space. The bedding was crisp white, which complemented the dark woods and gray walls. There was no baby furniture in the room yet, but there was a small pile of baby blankets folded on the bed, as though one of them had recently done laundry in preparation for their new arrival.

Inside the equally impressive walk-in closet, Ethan slid his nearly all black clothes to the side and pushed on the wall panel, which opened outward like a door. From the outside, there would have been no way for anyone to know it was there.

"There's a door to the finished basement and below ground storage next to the laundry room," he said, flipping the switch to turn on the light over a staircase that led down to the subterranean level. "But this safe room space isn't on any of the blueprints."

Following him down the stairs, I was impressed by the forethought it took to come up with the building plan for the hidden room.

When we reached the bottom, there was an open entryway with a steel door on the side wall. Ethan punched in a code that beeped in affirmation before the heavy door swung open with a hiss.

The air inside was cool and still, carrying the scent of concrete and metal. To the right was an open living area, already furnished with a sofa, television, and other pieces, as well as a small kitchen in the corner. The door to the bathroom and even a bedroom took up a side wall. Shelves lined with non-perishable food, medical supplies, and a few personal items lined the other side of the space. Directly to the back, a dark room was lit up by a bank of monitors, only a few with video feed running—silent sentinels keeping watch. It was clear the entire property wasn't under surveillance yet, which was why I was there, but he'd already done a lot of the work himself.

"There's an exit there," he said, pointing toward the door against the wall opposite us. "The tunnel takes you to a cave that pops out about a half of a mile to the east."

"This is outstanding, Ethan. I would have never expected this to be down here."

"If it hadn't been for the hidden basement in my other cabin, I don't know where Scarlett and I would be right now." A flicker of something I couldn't decipher passed through his light eyes with his admission, but it faded quickly. "It allowed us to get a head start when Victor's guys found us." He shook his head, as though forcing the memory away. "Caroline doesn't know about all of my...past. She's been through so much, after losing Daniel, and everything with Evie. So, if it comes up—"

"I get it," I assured him. Although I didn't understand everything he'd done in his life, or the ins and outs of the relationship he had with his sister, I knew what he needed from me, and it wasn't my place to share his truths with her. My job was to help him protect them—the fiercely independent sister who seemed to have already been through so much, the child whose laughter was a balm to the aches I didn't know I carried, his unborn chance at a new life, and the woman who had survived hell to find love again.

Following him, I stepped into the surveillance room. My hand hovered over the console, fingertips brushing against the cold buttons. "I can add layers to the security system—more cameras, including those with thermal imaging and motion sensors that signal when the passerby is over a certain body mass. There are many options."

Ethan nodded, his shoulders relaxing just a bit as he ran his fingers through his dark hair. "Good. After what we've already been through, I don't think we can be too cautious. I've already added security at Caroline's cottage as well, but hers will also need beefing up. There's nothing more important than protecting my family. I'd burn the world down before I let anything happen to them again."

The word *family* settled in my chest like a stone. My own family was a concept tangled in wires and distant memories because my parents were dead and I was an only child, but it didn't mean I couldn't understand how much this meant to Ethan. He and his family had taken me in without question, so although they weren't my blood, protecting them was just as important to me.

With a dip of my chin, I lowered myself into the desk chair and opened the browser on the computer. "Then let's make sure you never have to."

CHAPTER 4
The Phoenix

I was admittedly surprised when my brother invited the hacker, Tristan, not only to the bookstore, but to the home he shared with his pregnant wife. It told me one thing: Ethan trusted him, which was a rare gift he gave to anyone. Although I still wasn't privy to what he and my brother had gone through together, and how it involved Scarlett, I appreciated how much my brother had grown to trust anyone, because letting people in was never something he was willing to do...*until Scarlett.*

Leaving Scarlett and Ethan's house after the cookout, where Ethan and Tristan spent most of the evening surveying the property and planning for his new security system, I drove slowly down the mountain with Evie asleep in the backseat and Tristan in the passenger seat. He was so tall. I wasn't even sure how he fit in my sedan.

Although my brother had offered to drive his friend back to his hotel, I wouldn't hear of it. The hotel Tristan was staying in was only a few miles away from my cottage, so I had no problem bringing him back. The problem was I didn't know what to say to him on the twenty minute drive, so I tapped my fingers against the steering wheel, awkward as hell.

"So," he started, the pause that followed telling me he was just as unsure of what to say as I was. When I glanced toward him from the corner of my eye, he was looking out the window at the dense forest, the lights of the dashboard reflecting off his dark framed glasses. "Did you move here when Ethan and Scarlett moved or did you live here before or..."

Lowering the volume on the radio, I nodded, knowing the movement hadn't been enough for him to even notice it. "I...um...yes. We moved here to be near my brother."

He smiled as he turned his hazel eyes in my direction, and I couldn't deny how handsome he was—*young*, but handsome. He couldn't have been more than twenty-five, which was definitely too young for me to even pay attention, but I couldn't seem to help it. "The two of you must be close."

Although I wasn't sure if it was a question, I nodded again. "Our entire lives," I said, knowing there was no way to quantify how close my brother and I really were. He was everything to Evie and me. "After our parents died, and then after—" Pain seized my chest and the words got stuck in my throat. I blinked back the burn in my eyes, clearing my throat. "After Daniel passed, Ethan, Evie, and I became inseparable—not that we weren't close before. I'm not sure what we would have done without him."

A sad smile lifted the corner of my mouth as I turned to meet his stare, not expecting the grief struggling to tear through my chest to be mirrored in his expression. "I'm sorry, Caroline. I lost parents when I was young also, but Daniel...your husband? I can't imagine what that feels like."

His confession surprised me, and it suddenly became clearer why my brother had befriended this man. Although I still knew little about him, his nature was written all over his face. He may have been young, but he knew pain, and he knew grief. Ethan would never be able to find a true friend in someone who didn't, because it was pain and grief that had shaped so much of who he was, whether or not he was willing to admit it.

My shoulder lifted in a half-hearted shrug because I didn't know what else to do. There were moments when I allowed my grief to run free, but not now. "Thank you, and yes, he was my husband." Was. Is. I still hadn't figured out what it meant to be a widow. The platinum band on my left ring finger said to the world that I was very much still married, whether my husband was still with me or not.

Turning off the mountain road and onto the main highway, I changed the subject. "So...a hacker, huh? I admittedly do not know what exactly a hacker does."

He chuckled, the deep rumble of his voice sending a shiver down my spine that I wasn't brave enough to analyze. It had been an exceedingly long time since I'd been with a man, but it wasn't something I had any interest in. Still, it was normal for my body to respond to a handsome man who had a nice smile and even nicer voice—I hoped. "I'm not even sure sometimes. Basically, I'm just really good at lots of computer stuff, which means I make a living doing whatever my clients need me to do that involves technology."

We both knew there was plenty more he could divulge, but I didn't press further. Well, not completely. "I'm guessing it's not always legal, then." When his eyes grew wide and he went silent, I added to my question. "It's okay. I'm sure you know more about what my brother does than I do."

When the tension in his jaw released, I hoped that meant he was at least a little more at ease.

"I'm not so sure." He huffed a laugh as he turned to gaze back out the window, although there was nothing he could see in the darkness. "Your brother is a pretty private guy."

That was an understatement. I nodded. "That's the truth, but when you pull back the dark layers, he truly is an amazing person. I've never met anyone more loyal, generous, or protective over those he loves. He's surrounded by shadows, but there's light beneath them, and it's pure."

Once I dropped Tristan off at his hotel, I headed back home, carrying Evelyn's sleeping form inside. I truly did not know how a person could sleep so soundly through everything. It took an act of Congress and for the world to spin in reverse for me to fall asleep without some manner of medication, and even those weren't all that effective.

Standing in the doorway, I watched her for a few minutes, in complete awe of how beautiful she was, how perfect. Her blue eyes, that were closed with her long lashes fanned against her cheeks, were all mine, but so much of her was Daniel—the chestnut hair that had only just begun to grow back, and the scowl that twisted her lips every morning when she refused to take her medicine. It was at that moment, as I gazed down at the center of my universe, watching her chest rise and dip with each breath, that the armor surrounding my heart cracked and peeled open like a dam that had begun to lose its foundation, allowing the storm of emotion it had been struggling to hold back to pour through. Then, in the dark room where no one could see me crumble, I let the tears flow. For that one moment, as I caressed the cheek of the only thing that gave me no choice but to keep fighting, I allowed all the hopeless thoughts to flood my mind, wondering if after three years, I could survive one more day without him.

Sunlight shined in through the gauzy curtains of my bedroom the next morning far earlier than I wanted it to, but I didn't think it took requests. My eyelids felt like sand-paper as I blinked against the sun's intrusion. I tried to close them and roll back over, but my alarm started screaming before I even had the chance to change positions.

Tossing my blankets off, I groaned and reached for my phone, turning the alarm off. I was tired, but I was a mom, and Evie's shuffling footsteps told me she was already awake. A second later, big blue eyes met mine. "I'm hungry."

For the next hour, Evie and I went through our morning routine: breakfast, medicine, and getting ready for the day. To Evie's dismay, however, Ethan didn't make it for breakfast since new inventory had gotten delivered to the bookstore and Scarlett needed his help. She needed my help too, so I headed there right after dropping Evie off at school.

My mood instantly improved when I parked outside the small-town bookstore. After years, having a job was finally a way for me to take back a small part of my independence. It wasn't much, but I relished the chance to earn my own money and use my time to be a part of something for the future of our family. I wasn't a partner in the business, not really, but I took pride in it all the same.

Scarlett smiled at me as I walked inside, the line of customers at the cafe counter already several bodies deep. Knowing she needed me more than Ethan did, who was helping a customer by the stacks, I pulled my apron on and joined her behind the counter. "Good morning."

Handing the older gentleman in front of her his coffee, Scarlett turned her deep brown eyes to me and smiled again. She truly was a stunning woman. Pregnancy looked good on her. "Good morning to you. It's been like this since we opened the door this morning."

I dipped my chin at our other employee, a college student named Jules, and took over making a latte so Scarlett could focus on the register. "I see that. They must know its inventory day."

So busy making coffee and keeping up with the cafe side of the store, I hadn't noticed the tall, handsome man who'd entered the store when I wasn't looking.

Dressed in jeans, a gray flannel with the sleeves rolled up, and a band T-shirt underneath, Tristan looked totally out of place—just like my brother. His hazel eyes met mine across the room and I had five seconds to decide if I was going to smile or look busy, so I opted for the awkward combination of both. If I ever did decide to date again, I would need a training course or something, because I was way out of practice.

Seeming to take my half smile and pretend busyness as an invitation, he made a beeline for the counter, a genuine smile spreading across his face. "Good morning, Scarlett... Caroline."

The steam wand I was using to make a latte decided to explode foamy milk across the top of my apron at that very moment. I'd seen enough porn to know exactly what that looked like, and I wasn't surprised when he and Scarlett both stifled a laugh before Scarlett reached over and handed me a rag.

"Thanks," I grumbled, doing my best to wipe the milky white substance off my apron but all I did was smear it.

"Grab another apron from the back," Scarlett said, but I was already moving, tossing my apron down on the edge of the counter and pulling a new one off the hook.

By the time I returned to the front, Tristan was already gone, standing near the back of the store with my brother. His eyes met mine when I looked his way, however, and the side of his lips lifted in the shy sort of smile that sent my heart into a flip. It had been a long time since someone looked at me that way, and I really didn't know how I felt about it. I smiled back but returned to my task, doing my best to focus on making an espresso for the woman in front of me who appeared less than patient. By the next day, I knew he would return to his home in Atlanta, and I would stay behind in my own little, small-town bubble, just the way I liked it. It wasn't like I was lonely or anything. At least that was what I told myself.

CHAPTER 5

The Phantom

The night swallowed the sound of Caroline's car engine as she disappeared around the bend, leaving me alone in the darkened street. I stayed outside the hotel for a moment, breathing in the pine-scented air. It was so much colder in the mountains after dark—lonelier—when there was no one around but the stars. Unlike in the city, the quiet night was eerie, especially with how the mist curled its way around the tree roots and headstones of the cemetery a few blocks away. A shiver raced through me that had nothing to do with the cold, sending me retreating into my hotel room.

Once I was inside, I sat on the edge of the bed, taking off my glasses and rubbing my fingers over my eyes. Caroline's face haunted the shadows of the room—just the thought of how widowhood must press down on her every day, how devastating it must be. Still, there was such resilience in her eyes. Being a widow may have fractured her, but being a mother clearly kept her whole. And Evie... Her snaggle-toothed smile was a reminder of how life persisted amidst the cruel grip of cancer, and just looking at her could make your soul smile. They were both so fucking strong, and it was truly awe-inspiring.

Grief knotted in my chest as I thought of Daniel's untimely departure from the world, leaving Caroline and Evie to navigate their complicated life without him. It was a familiar ache, one that mirrored the emptiness in my own life, although my parents had been gone for a long time. The loss of someone who meant the world to you was not something you could ever truly get over.

Running my hand through my hair, I sighed and slid my glasses back on. The silence was heavy, charged with my obligations to Ethan and his family. His trust was a sacred thing, and I could not let him down. I had promised him that I would help to keep them safe, and now my mind was in complete turmoil about how to do it. My skill set allowed me to hack systems—to lay the secrets of the dark web bare and bring powerful people to their knees—but there was no firewall against the unpredictability of the mob's vengeance. The very idea of guaranteeing anyone's safety against them felt like trying to hold smoke—slippery, elusive, impossible. The Barrilleaux family had become like my own family, their struggles woven with my own existence, but I did not know how to protect them when every shadow could be an enemy.

"Damn it," I muttered into the quiet room as I stood, my breath fogging the cool window as I stepped in front of it. The streetlight changed to green, but there were no cars at the intersection. Everyone had already gone home for the night, already tucked safely into their beds. Life went on for everyone else in the small town, not knowing the dangers that threatened the young family that had just opened the bookshop on Main Street. Until the case was settled, their lives would be clouded by uncertainty. Still, this family knit together by tragedy and a fiercely loyal love was not one to break easily. Their strength was something to be admired. So, even though tendrils of doubt crept through my mind and made my knees buckle, it was Ethan's devotion to his family that hardened my resolve.

The bell above the door chimed softly as I stepped into the quaint little bookstore. The scent of old paper and ink mingled with the warm aroma of freshly brewed coffee, wrapping around me like a comforting embrace. They did not have places like this in Atlanta—not anywhere near my apartment anyway. My eyes immediately met Caroline's baby blues from across the room, where she was standing behind the machine used to make lattes. She smiled at me but turned away quickly, a pretty flush staining her cheeks as she returned to the task at hand. Glancing at where Ethan was still helping a customer, I headed toward the cafe counter to where Scarlett and Caroline were working, taking up the place from where the last customer vacated.

"Good morning, Scarlett...Caroline."

Scarlett looked up at me, the warmth in her smile reflecting in her deep brown eyes. "Morning, Tristan. How'd you sleep?"

"Better than I expected," I lied. My thoughts from the night before still lingered at the edge of my mind, but I pushed them down for the moment. "What about you?"

"Like a rock," she said, her eyes crinkling at the corners as she grinned. "I think all that fresh mountain air wore me out."

"Can't argue with that." From the corner of my eye, I stole a glance at Caroline, who was focused intently on her task of creating intricate patterns in the foam atop someone's coffee. She was about to speak, but as in a twist of fate, a wayward plume of foamed milk erupted from the pitcher Caroline held, splattering across her apron, drawing all three of our attention. Her expression morphed into one of mild exasperation. I tried not to chuckle, but all five-foot-barely-anything of her was fucking adorable, so the smile spread across my face before I could stop it.

Reaching below the counter, Scarlett grabbed a rag and handed it to Caroline, who took it gladly, a flush crawling up her neck and to darken her cheeks as her eyes flicked to me. "Thanks." With her attempts to clean herself failing, she headed toward the back of the store, untying her apron as she went. I shamelessly watched her walk away, taking in every charming inch of her—every nuance.

"Grab another apron from the back," Scarlett said, turning her smile back to me, her eyes sparkling with amusement.

"Here you go. Try not to make any more messes. Are you heading back home today?"

"Hey, that wasn't my fault!" A playful smirk tugged up the side of my lips as I took the mug of coffee, savoring the rich aroma. When I pulled the coffee away from my lips, I nodded. "Yeah. I need to get back home to my cat, but I'll be back when the rest of the equipment is in."

Scarlett smiled at someone behind me, and I turned to look over my shoulder as Ethan approached me from behind. "Well, when you come back next time, maybe you should bring your cat along. Evie would love that."

"Tristan," Ethan said, grabbing my attention. "I have something to give you in the office before you head out."

Taking one more look in the direction Caroline disappeared in, I turned and followed Ethan toward the office at the back of the store. When we got there, he slid a built-in bookshelf to the side, revealing a safe behind it, opened it quickly and pulled out a small object: *a thumb drive.*

"Everything Scarlett's father had on Victor's gang is on here. *Everything.* I have copies of it as well, so you can take this one. Guard it with your life and do whatever you have to do with this information to keep my family—and yourself—safe."

I nodded, my chest notably tight as I reached out and took the small black item out of his hand, sliding it into a zipped pocket of my laptop case. "I will start going over everything tonight and will let you know what I find."

With one more look of understanding between us, we headed back toward the front counter, where Scarlett was still standing by the register, and Caroline had returned, her eyes flicking up to meet mine.

"Your help...it means more than you know," Scarlett said, stepping around the counter to hug me.

When she finally let me go, I turned to Caroline, who stood a little apart, although her eyes seemed to miss nothing. "And you... keep being the rock star that you are and tell the little Captain that I will see her later, alligator."

Caroline nodded, a sweet smile gracing her full lips. "Take care of yourself, Tristan. Hope to see you again soon."

It was midday by the time I stepped back into my downtown Atlanta apartment, but with every shade pulled down behind black curtains, you could have sworn it was night. The click of the lock echoed, a sharp reminder of the solitude that awaited within its walls. But as I stepped further into the room, a sleek black shape unfurled from the corner of the gray sofa, reminding me I wasn't alone after all.

"Houdini." I smiled as my cat sauntered over, his tail high as he swirled around my legs, purring in welcome. Closing the door behind me, I dropped my bags to the ground and stooped over to scratch behind his ears. "I missed you too, buddy."

"Come on," I murmured, watching the loading bar inch across the screen of my center monitor. After my long drive back to Atlanta, I'd fallen asleep on the couch with Houdini curled up on my lap, but with the sky outside now dark, I was anxious to give Ethan some sort of update.

First checking the tracking on the shipment of security hardware Ethan and I had ordered from his safe room, I was at least relieved most of it was enroute to his property. A fortress was only as strong as its weakest point, and I refused to let their defenses falter on my watch. I wasn't yet sure what dark tide was rising around them, but I needed them to be prepared to defend against it.

Perched beside me on the desk, Houdini's tail twitched as though he was just as impatient with me as I was. I reached across the desk, scratching behind his ear. "Alright, buddy. It's time to find some answers." Even with the gravity of the situation, I couldn't help but smile as he leaned into my touch.

The hum of the cooling fan blended with the distant sound of traffic outside my window as my fingers moved across the keyboard, Houdini settling in beside me. He was already snoring by the time I accessed the hidden forum known as "The Underbelly." It was a digital cesspool where criminals of all sorts gathered to exchange information, sell contraband, and plan things that would give most warm-blooded creatures nightmares. I'd stumbled into the forum purely by accident two years earlier when trying to keep a well-known state politician out of hot water for tax fraud and had been finding lots of useful information in there ever since.

Like a ghost, I passed right through layers of encryption, each one more complex than the last, hoping to find my way into the places where Victor Delacroix's remaining gang members lingered. With their leader dead and gone, however, there was a real chance they'd gone so far underground that I would not even be able to find them, but I wasn't ready to give up on myself just yet.

With my focus homed in on the task at hand, I sifted through the idle chatter and endless plotting for the rare kernels of truth to be found in such a place. Even after death, Victor Delacroix's name was a specter that loomed large in such circles—his gang's tendrils entwined deep within the city's foundation for decades, and with his gang conducting illegal trading with entities both at home and abroad, it was not unheard of to find his name in channels from outside of New Orleans as well.

Prowling through posts and back channels, I hunted for anything that might shed light on the FBI's case against Victor's gang, but it was like searching for a needle in a haystack.

And then there it was, stark against the dark background—a post from someone called ShadowRunner.

"Insider info on FBI's Delacroix case," read the title, and my pulse quickened. It wasn't just another breadcrumb. This promised to be the loaf. I'd already spent time going through the thumb drive Ethan had given to me, but I hadn't found anything on there that would be of use just yet. I intended to dig further, but this was a real lead, or a very convenient ploy. It was clear ShadowRunner was speaking with the confidence of the truly knowledgeable, or the foolishly bold. Although the communication wasn't meant for me, but possibly for members of Delacroix's gang who were undoubtedly willing to pay for the information, I hijacked the communication under an alternate alias of Sentinel. My moniker of Phantom was me at my core—able to slip through the net of cyberspace unnoticed, untraceable—but even shadows feared exposure when they encountered something darker. I realized this ShadowRunner could be a beacon or a trap, but they were the only lead I had at the moment. Not knowing ShaddowRunner's intentions, however, I didn't want them to know my main alias.

"Need details on Etienne's part," I typed, my fingers almost betraying the urgency that clawed at my insides. "Time sensitive."

With a click, the message disappeared into the ether, and I leaned back in my chair, rubbing my eyes. I was already getting tired again. The cursor blinked on the screen, silently taunting me.

Refusing to let it win, I opened another tab. I'd gone through all the relevant news articles before, but just in case I'd missed something. I knew I was just distracting myself. Either way, I felt the need to read through them again.

Surprisingly, even looking a second and third time, I saw Scarlett's father's name in none of the articles about what happened in the distillery. If the feds knew about his involvement, they were keeping it close to the vest. The good thing was that, with Scarlett's father's name not being in the news in relation to Delacroix's death, neither was hers.

As I scrolled through the endless mentions of Victor Delacroix's death by every news channel south of the Mason-Dixon Line, a notification chimed from the other window I had left open in my browser—the chime cutting through the silence and causing Houdini to roll over from where he lounged across my desk.

Blowing out a breath, I flipped back to the other tab to see a message from ShadowRunner. A rush of adrenaline surged through me as I leaned forward in my chair, opening the correspondence. "Information comes at a price, Sentinel, but I trust you understand the stakes."

I went quiet for a moment, understanding more about the stakes than even ShadowRunner did. What I didn't know was what he would want in exchange for the information—whether he was offering it up because he wanted to see the mobsters behind bars, or whether he wanted to see Scarlett's father dead. At the end of the day, however, I wouldn't know unless I bit.

"Speak," I typed back, the word concise and commanding even though my pulse hammered a frantic rhythm at my temples.

For several moments, I watched the flickering screen, hoping whatever he sent back was worth something.

Finally, after I thought he may have disappeared altogether, the message unfurled across the screen. "Ivy Etienne is under the watchful eye of the feds, and Delacroix's boys are more than aware. They're looking for him, but he's safe. *For now*. Witness protection until the trial sings its verdict—unless his enemies find him first."

CHAPTER 6

The Phoenix

Tristan's absence was not missed by my very perceptive daughter when I picked her up from school the day he left, but, just like any other seven-year-old, her attention quickly shifted as she poured the contents of her backpack out in the backseat of the car to tell me all about her science project. It was her first time going to a real school in a long time, and she was loving it. The opportunity to use a thousand craft supplies was like Christmas morning, so it was all she talked about the entire way home—Tristan temporarily forgotten.

Once we got home, Evie immediately spread her supplies out on the kitchen table, foam balls rolling onto the floor. I scooped them up before making her a snack of sliced strawberries. She climbed into the chair, her small, delicate fingers wrapped around the glue stick. Her other hand lifted a strawberry to her mouth, her eyes wide with excitement. "Mommy, do you think we should use glitter on Earth, so it's super special?"

Sliding the glitter across the table, I nodded." I think that's a great idea, nugget... lots of glitter."

Eve giggled, her laughter like music to my ears. It was hard to believe that less than a year ago, she had been so sick, fighting for her life. Now, here she was, full of energy and joy, lighting up the room with her presence.

Her tongue peeked out the corner of her mouth as she coated the blue planet in glue and then dipped it in colorful glitter. In that moment, as I ruffled the soft fuzz on her scalp and the golden rays of the sunset reflected in her eyes, I let myself believe in the normalcy we were painstakingly creating. It was almost too perfect, and I was afraid to blink and have it all fall away. As I watched her work, the doorbell chimed, disrupting my thoughts.

Leaving Evie at the table, I walked to the front door, expecting to see Ethan and Scarlett standing on my front porch since they were coming over for dinner. Instead, my eyes landed on the face of a delivery man holding a package.

"Oh, hey," I said, taking the stylus from him to sign on the pad.

He smiled, holding the box out for me to take it, but my attention was drawn over his shoulder. A few houses down, and on the opposite side of the street, a black SUV sat parked on its shoulder. It was clear there was someone inside, but I couldn't see their features from where I was standing. Something about the vehicle's presence sent a shiver of unease down my spine, but when I turned my attention back to the delivery man, the mysterious vehicle drove away, the tinted windows too dark for me to see inside as they passed by.

"Have a good day," the delivery driver said, glancing over his shoulder to follow my line of sight before walking back to his vehicle.

Coming from the opposite direction, Scarlett's SUV appeared from around the curve, headlights cutting through the darkening street between us. I set the box down just inside the front door, but remained outside, wrapping my arms around my chest as I watched them pull into the driveway. The moment I saw my brother's smile, a matching one spread across my lips, the unease dissipating, at least for the moment.

With my belly pleasantly full of Scarlett's jambalaya, Ethan and I moved to sit on the back porch while Scarlett took Evie for her bath. There was no doubt she would be an amazing mother. Scarlett had a naturally kind demeanor, and my daughter fell in love with her from the moment she'd met her. We all did.

A million stars sparkled in the sky as I gazed up, holding my mug of tea with both hands. Ethan sat beside me, staring up at the same sky.

"Beautiful up here," he said, the tone of his voice pensive.

After a lifetime together, I always knew when he had something on his mind, but I also knew not to push for more. When he was ready to spill whatever was on his mind, he would.

I nodded, taking a sip, and closing my eyes as the hot liquid slid down my throat. "It is. It's a different life here...slower."

In the corner of my eye, I saw him nod. "But you like it here? You don't regret moving?"

Suddenly, I had a better idea of what was on his mind. Guilt maybe? But there was no reason for him to feel guilty.

The side of my mouth tipped up in a grin as I shook my head. "Not at all. I didn't leave anything more behind than you did... nothing but broken dreams and bad memories."

Turning my eyes away from the sky, my smile fell slightly. "Why do you ask? Do you regret leaving?"

The side-eye he sent my way made me huff a laugh, but I didn't respond, waiting for him to answer my question.

Blowing out a breath, he leaned back in his chair. "No. Leaving New Orleans was necessary for us to start over—for me to give Scarlett the life she deserved. I'll never regret that."

I nodded, looking back up at the sky. With the light pollution in New Orleans, it was impossible to see the stars. Evie deserved to see the stars.

"Is that because of her ex?" Even in the dark, I didn't miss the way his jaw clenched. Ethan had always kept what he told me on a 'need-to-know' basis, so I made it a habit of not asking questions. I knew all he ever wanted to do was keep us safe, but we were both adults, so I also knew I could handle more than what he chose to divulge. "You never did tell me what all happened there, and I normally don't ask, but..."

For a long moment, there was silence between us, the only sounds coming from critters somewhere in the trees.

The air seemed to become thinner as anxiety squeezed my lungs with every second I waited for him to respond.

Finally, when I'd nearly given up on getting a response at all, he shifted in his seat, and I knew he was going to talk.

"Her husband was only part of the equation." Ethan's gaze cut through the moonlit darkness, sharp and penetrating. "I was sent to kill her, Cara, by her own husband."

The revelation struck like a physical blow, twisting my stomach into knots. There was so much I wanted to know, like how close he had come to actually fulfilling the task, but I was afraid to ask, because I was afraid of the answer. My mouth, on the other hand, seemed to have other plans. "You were... What?" I managed to choke out, my vocal cords like sandpaper.

He blew out a breath, the turmoil in his eyes mirroring what tightened my own chest. "Joshua Prejean hired me to end her. But when I saw her..." As though shame prevented him from saying anymore, Ethan's eyes flicked away, his head moving in a nearly unperceivable shake. "But when I saw her, something shifted inside me. I couldn't do it. I just couldn't. He was already killing her. He was a monster. I had to save her from him—to take her away from that life." Looking up at the sky, his voice softened. "Even though he did everything he could to snuff her light out, she burned so bright—just like the stars. She deserved so much more. She still does."

"Does she know?" The question clawed its way up my throat, although I hoped I already knew the answer. I hoped Scarlett hadn't been left in the dark.

Ethan nodded, a silent affirmation that held a thousand confessions he would never speak aloud. "She knows everything. I don't keep things about her life from her."

A whirlwind of emotions tore through me: relief, horror, admiration. Through it all, one truth remained: Ethan had risked everything, defying the nature of the person he'd been for so long, to pull Scarlett from the abyss. No matter how much darkness lived in him, he was a good man.

For the next hour, Ethan told me the heartbreaking story of Scarlett's past in more detail, and more about what had brought them into each other's lives—the twist of fate that could have made life so different from how it turned out.

Even though my brother never explained where the money came from over the years, I always knew it was blood money. After our parents died when I was only eighteen, I petitioned the state to take on the custody of my younger brother, and they obliged. We had no other family, and at sixteen, he was too old to be adopted. I was a better choice than a halfway house. And although I'd given it my all to take care of him and keep him out of trouble, I knew I could never be a mother figure to him. We were siblings, and barely two years apart, so I wasn't any more capable of taking care of him than he was of taking care of himself. I knew when he'd started hanging out with questionable people that his life was heading in a direction that would tarnish his soul, but I'd been merely a kid myself, and Ethan had a mind of his own. The more I'd tried to rein him in, the more he'd pulled away. We had grown closer over the years, through shared grief and trauma, but my brother unquestionably had literal skeletons in his closet, and that sent my stomach into a tumble.

"Are you worried about retaliation?" I asked after several long heartbeats as I tried to process everything he'd told me.

A muscle in his jaw flexed as he nodded, the one way to know when he was feeling the pressure. "That was why I had Tristan come here. I don't trust just anyone with the safety of my family, especially when we're trying to keep Scarlett off the radar. If they find out where she is, I don't know what they'll do, and I can't take that chance."

The admission chilled my blood. Knowing how good of a person Scarlett was, I couldn't imagine her going through the hell she'd already been through. It wasn't fair that, after everything, she would be targeted by those who wanted to get back at her father. "And Tristan, he knows everything? Are you sure you can trust him?"

Although I felt in my core that I already knew the answer, I still asked. I hadn't spent much time with Tristan, but it had been enough to know he was genuine.

Ethan's nod confirmed. "If it wasn't for him, we would be in a very different place right now."

No matter how much I knew he had done for Scarlett, a protective wave surged through my chest, like a mother bear roused to defend her cub. "Are we safe, Ethan? Will Evie be safe?"

"I killed Delacroix, her husband's accomplice, and her husband is dead." Even with fallen enemies, Ethan's jaw clenched, telling me he was still worried. "But their shadows may linger. I'm not foolish enough to believe they won't look for revenge, but I don't know if there are any supporters of Delacroix left who even know Scarlett was involved in what happened all those months ago. They may know about her father, but not about her. That's my hope, anyway."

Turning toward me, he reached out and took my hand. "I know what we're up against if they seek retribution. I've already gone up against Delacroix's gang, and I've fought against darker demons than even them. I didn't emerge from that world to stand by and watch it claim the ones I love. I'll do whatever it takes to keep our family safe. This is something I promise you, Cara. You, Evie, Scarlett, and my baby."

The last of the evening's dishes clinked softly against each other as I set them on the drying rack. Down the hall, Evie slept soundly, but for some reason, my heart thudded discordantly against the peacefulness of our cottage.

Hands dripping and pruned, I turned the faucet off, a chill running down my spine as my eyes locked onto the black SUV parked across the street. The lights in my neighbor's house were off. The SUV wasn't directly in front of their house but in between our two properties. I didn't know why it was there, but it cast an ominous shadow underneath the moonlit sky that filled me with dread.

Air seized in my lungs as I stared at the dark vehicle through the reflection of myself in the glass, my heartbeat speeding up.

"Get a hold of yourself, Caroline," I whispered to myself, trying to shake off the unease that settled deep in my chest. Ever since Ethan told me about Scarlett's haunting past the night before, and about everything they'd gone through together, my mind had been filled with thoughts of danger lurking in the shadows, ready to strike when I least expected it. The SUV could have been for someone visiting the elderly couple who lived across the street, but what if it wasn't? What if a ghost of my brother and Scarlett's past dealings had found its way to our doorstep, looking for retribution or leverage? What if we were just easy prey? A shiver danced across my shoulders, and I wrapped my arms around myself, needing comfort.

Moving away from the window, my feet were silent against the hardwood floor as I started my nightly ritual of making sure the house was secured before bed. Although we no longer lived in a city ripe with crime, it still seemed like a good habit to hang onto.

Evie's soft breathing was the sole sound of peace in the deafening quiet that blanketed our home. As I turned the deadbolt on the front door, doubt gnawed at me like a persistent itch, making me wonder if I should call my brother, but I couldn't rouse the sleeping beast without a good reason. Ethan had seen too much darkness, and he didn't need shadows cast by my fraying nerves. Each window's lock met my touch with steadfast resistance, offering silent promises of safety. Yet, for every latch secured, my mind drew tighter, strung like a bow waiting to strike at an unknown threat.

When I returned to the kitchen, I leaned my forehead against the cool glass of the kitchen window, peering out into darkness where shadows clung to the edges of the world. I searched for the SUV, but it had vanished like a phantom, leaving only the ghost of a presence behind. You would think its disappearance would have soothed the tension in my shoulders, but the unease remained, a stubborn knot in my gut refusing to be untangled by logic or reason.

"Mommy?" Evie's tiny voice cut through the silence. I jerked upright, heart seizing for a panicked moment.

"You should be asleep, nugget." Leaving the window behind, I rushed to her side, cursing the fear that made my voice sharper than intended. The last thing I wanted was to worry her.

Eyes barely holding open, she held the stuffed llama tightly in one arm, wrapping the other around my leg. "I had a bad dream. Can you sleep with me?"

Without another thought, I nodded, rubbing my hand against her back. I understood nightmares all too well. "Absolutely, sweetheart. Let's get you back to bed."

CHAPTER 7
The Phoenix

"Can we get ice cream after this, mommy? Chocolate chip. No...cotton candy!" Evie's tiny voice broke me out of my thoughts, her depthless ocean eyes were watching me and waiting for a response. I'd been dwelling on the mysterious black SUV all day, wondering if I should tell my brother, but convincing myself that I was being ridiculous. It was probably someone just visiting a neighbor, or even someone using the street for one of the many hiking trails that branched off it. There were a thousand reasons why a vehicle could be parked on my street, but something about it rubbed me the wrong way. Paranoid. With how bad my depression and anxiety had been as of late, I couldn't give the question any more weight over me than it already had.

Forcing a smile onto my face, I nodded. "Anything you want, nugget."

With the last vial filled, the nurse withdrew the needle and placed a Minnie Mouse bandage over Evie's wound. "Let me go get Dr. Warner, so you can get that ice cream."

A bright smile spread across Evie's face as the nurse left, her missing front tooth only making her cuter.

"Maybe afterwards," I begin, grabbing her tiny hand and wrapping my fingers around it, "we can go to the bookstore and see Aunt Scarlett and Uncle Ethan."

As expected, my daughter's smile brightened. "Yes. Yes. Yes. I'm ready for my baby cousin to be born already."

Her smile instantly fell, her lower lip puffing out into a pout. Ever since she met Scarlett, Evie had been obsessed with her new aunt, and once she found out about Scarlett's pregnancy, it was all she could talk about.

"Not much longer, and then you will be the best cousin...I mean *auntie* in the whole world." Although I was aware Evie would be the baby's cousin, she'd been so enamored with Scarlett ever since they'd met, that she insisted on being called the new baby's 'auntie,' so we'd let her run with it.

For a moment, Evie basked in the praise, giddy with excitement for the new baby, but then Dr. Warner walked in, and her smile fell a little. She was much too young to go through what she'd already gone through, but she still handled it with bravery and sass.

"How are we doing today, Miss Evelyn?" The look on the doctor's face gave the tension in my chest permission to release, if only a little.

Setting her file down on the counter—her very thick file—he washed his hands before turning back to face us.

"Guess what," Evie said, her voice low and wispy, as though she was about to spill a secret.

The doctor leaned in, his eyebrow lifting as he placed the stethoscope against her chest. "What?"

Taking a deep breath as he instructed, her smile went wide again. "I'm gonna be an auntie soon and her name is Adelaide and she's going to be my best friend."

The words tumbled out like a dam bursting, nearly too fast for me to keep up. After the last syllable hit the air, she lifted her hand to her mouth, covering it and giggling. She really was the cutest kid.

Once he had finished listening to her lungs, Dr. Warner pressed his fingers along her neck, checking her lymph nodes to make sure they weren't enlarged. The prodding didn't seem to bother her, however. After two years of cancer treatments, she'd grown used to it. "Well, that is very exciting indeed, Miss Evelyn. Are you going to let her play with your dolls?"

Evie went quiet for a moment, her face turning pensive, as she thought on the subject. "Maybe when she's bigger, mister doctor. Did you know that babies put everything into their mouths?" Her lips pursed as though she was disgusted by the thought. "I don't want her eating my babies. "

Dr. Warner chuckled, his eyes crinkling beneath bushy gray eyebrows. "I think that's a good decision. Maybe you can buy her a doll just for babies."

Clapping her hands together, Evie nodded and turned to look at me. "Can we, mommy? Please. Please. Please."

Joy warmed my insides from her excitement. Nodding, I adjusted the pink cap on her head, covering where thick chestnut locks used to be. Her hair would grow back, though, slowly but surely. "We sure can. I think she would love that."

Memories of Evie being a baby in Daniel's arms flooded into my mind, the back of my eyes burning. I only let them linger for a moment before pushing the tears back, not wanting her to see my sadness and think it was because of her.

Picking up her file, the doctor made a few notes on the top page. "Well, Miss Evie, everything looks great today. As of now, your treatments seem to be working."

Relief flooded through my body, drowning out the grief that had dimmed my light all morning. "That's great news, Dr. Warner. Thank you."

We left the doctor's office not long afterward, with instructions to return in one month.

Getting back to the car, I strapped Evie into the backseat and then hopped into the driver's side. "All right, nugget. Ice cream is coming right up."

Pulling up at Tangled in the Pages Two, I was happy to see Ethan's car parked in the parking lot beside Scarlett's.

"Ready to go inside, nugget?"

In the rearview mirror, I could see Evelyn wiggling in her seat, her smile wide as she fumbled with her seatbelt. "Yes. Yes. Yes. I want to play with the train set!"

The early summer heat was stifling as I stepped out of the car, even though we were much farther north than where we'd always lived. It wasn't as hot as Louisiana, but I still couldn't imagine how hot it would be in August.

The bell over the door jingled when we walked inside, the scent of fresh brewed coffee hitting my nostrils. Scarlett and Ethan stood near the cafe, Scarlett's hand on her pregnant belly as they spoke in hushed voices. A few customers were scattered around the store, some browsing the shelves and others sitting down as they drank coffee or flipped through a magazine.

Running right past me, Evie wrapped her arms around Ethan's waist, bringing their conversation to a grinding halt. "Uncle Ethan! Mommy and I got ice cream!"

A bright grin spread across Ethan's face as he leaned over and scooped her up, giving her a kiss on the cheek. "And you didn't bring us any?"

Evie giggled and squirmed out of his arms. "You're silly, Uncle Ethan! It would have melted!"

Not waiting for a response, she darted toward the kids' section of the store, undoubtedly heading for the toy train.

"How was the appointment?" Scarlett asked, sliding a cup of coffee across the counter to one of our elderly regulars.

With a smile toward Harold when he walked past me, I pulled my apron off the hook and tied it around my waist before joining her behind the café counter. "It went well. He said she is still in remission, and that the meds seem to still be working."

A bright smile spread across my brother's face as he leaned over the counter to hug me. It was still strange to see him in such a domesticated role, owning and working in a bookstore, but I admittedly loved it. "We should go out tonight and celebrate."

For the next few hours, I dove into work, taking over café duty while Scarlett worked at the register. With the number of toys in the kids' section of the store, I never needed a babysitter. Evie could play for hours while I worked.

Once we left the store, the four of us piled into Scarlett's SUV and headed to our favorite local pizza place, by request of Evie, ordering dessert first as she insisted. With everything she'd been through, we all found telling her '*no*' to be impossible, a fact she had come to take advantage of. I didn't blame her. Children shouldn't have to spend their lives in hospital beds with tubes connected to their little bodies, pumping them full of poison. She learned at an early age that life wasn't fair.

"I spoke to Phantom earlier today," Ethan said, taking a sip of his draft beer. The name caught my attention, although I knew him by another name: *Tristan*.

"Oh?" was my only response, but I was admittedly curious as to when Tristan would return to our small piece of the world.

Swallowing a mouthful of pizza, I waited for Ethan to continue, but he glanced around us instead, undoubtedly making sure we weren't in earshot of anyone who could potentially hear our conversation. Thankfully, the restaurant was nearly empty. I glanced beside Ethan at Scarlett, her expression telling me that she already knew the details of the phone call, and that the information made her uncomfortable.

Ethan's eyes scanned the room again before they landed back on me. "The feds are preparing their case against the remaining members of Victor Delacroix's gang, and with Scarlett's father in protective custody, I can't guarantee that his family members won't end up in the same boat."

A cold chill crept down my spine at the thought of what that could mean for us—*for Evie*. The last thing I wanted was to thrust her into another situation she had no control over. The last thing I wanted was to make her leave her home when we'd only just built a new one. "Are you thinking we will have to go into protective custody as well?"

Although Ethan shrugged and took another sip of his beer, I could tell by the tension in his jaw that he wasn't completely unfazed by the prospect.

Scarlett shifted in her chair, her hand sliding protectively over her stomach. Soon, Evie wouldn't be the only child in our family that needed protecting, and we all knew that.

"What's protective custody, Mommy?"

Evie's question made me cringe, and I saw the same reaction on Ethan and Scarlett's faces.

Reaching over, I rubbed Evie's head. Her hair had a long way to go before it grew back to how it had been before her cancer, but feeling those fine strands between my fingers still made me smile. They reminded me that she was getting better.

"Well, my little Nosy-Rosie, you just reminded Mommy of how much your little ears hear, and just how clever you are."

Seeming to have already forgotten about her question, she grinned, her slice of cheese pizza hanging out of her mouth and dribbling grease down her chin.

It was clear Ethan had more he needed to say, however, and Scarlett seemed to realize it too, so she stood from the table and walked around to Evie's side. "Let's go look at the fish aquarium, munchkin. I hear they have some new babies in there."

Eyes lighting up, Evie jumped up from her chair, taking Scarlett's hand and allowing her aunt to lead her away.

The moment they were out of ear shot, Ethan blew out a breath. "It's possible. The one thing we have going for us is that, at least as of now, and from what our sources believe, the feds don't know about Scarlett's abduction months ago. This should prevent her from having to testify. However, what was left of her ex-husband was found at the scene, which could cause her to be dragged in anyway, even if they don't believe she knows anything. Also, we don't know if the remaining members of Victor's gang know about us, or whether or not they will seek retribution."

After dinner, Evie and I rode with Scarlett and Ethan back to the bookstore and hopped into my car, heading to our home as they went to theirs. The general tone of the night, at least for me, had somehow shifted. I loved my little cottage, as did Evie. We loved everything about it. But something nagged at me, even as I climbed into bed that night—even as I tried to ignore it, there was a fear inside me that wouldn't abate, something telling me that we weren't safe. I realized it may have just been paranoia, but the mysterious black SUV that I'd seen parked outside my house a few times over the past several days didn't help. With everything my little family had gone through, I certainly wasn't someone who walked around with rose-colored glasses, but the voice in the back of my head told me there was more to it than that. It told me there was something I needed to be afraid of, even when all I wanted to believe was that Evie and I were finally safe.

Needing to do something, I climbed out of bed and turned on my bedroom light, removing the shadows that could have been hiding monsters. When I looked out the kitchen window, the SUV wasn't there, but it didn't ease my paranoia. So instead of going back to sleep, I made my way around my small home, checking the locks on the doors and windows before double checking the alarm system. Everything appeared to be secure, but when I returned to my bedroom, unease still crept along my spine like the legs of a spider, sneaking up on me and ready to bite.

Glancing toward my bedroom door, I bit the corner of my thumbnail, trying to convince myself that I was just being silly, but my mind knew better. Unable to shake the feeling, I blew out a breath and rose from my bed again. I knew I wasn't going to be able to settle with how I felt, so I left my bedroom and went into Evie's room down the hall, scooping her up.

With my little girl in my arms, I went back into my bedroom and laid her down on my bed, grateful she did not wake up. After checking the hallway again and leaving the lights on, I closed my bedroom door and locked us inside. I knew I was probably going overboard, but I didn't care. The update Ethan revealed at dinner seemed to have burrowed itself into my subconscious, making me sense things that probably weren't there. I needed to know we were safe, so if I had to sleep with mace under my pillow and a child who slept like an octopus in my bed, then so be it.

Fast asleep on my bed, Evie's tiny frame was lost amid a sea of plush blankets and satin sheets. I brushed a kiss on her forehead, her skin cool and fragile beneath my lips.

"Goodnight, sweet girl," I murmured, but my heart was pounding wildly against my ribcage, a staccato rhythm fueled by fear.

Retreating to my bathroom, I splashed cold water on my face, trying to quell the rising tide of panic. In the mirror, the reflection looking back at me had eyes that flickered with shadows not cast by the room. My mind raced, cataloging the sounds of the house—the hum of the air conditioner, the distant drone of crickets, and the soft breaths of my daughter asleep just a wall away.

"Caroline, you can't fall apart right now," I whispered to myself, gripping the edge of the sink.

As the minutes ticked by, the weight of responsibility settled heavily on my shoulders. Ethan and Scarlett deserved their slice of happiness, unmarred by the darkness that seemed to follow our family like a relentless storm. I couldn't bring myself to shatter their newlywed bliss with my own fears, not until I knew those fears were grounded in reality. The last thing I wanted to do was call them in the middle of the night with nonsense, but the longer I stood there, the more uneasy I became.

Pushing my desk chair against the door and wedging its back under the doorknob, I let out a breath and reached for my phone. I stared at the dark screen for a few minutes before I dialed my brother's number, and then Scarlett's, but neither of them answered, only thinning the air more. They always answered the phone. *Always.*

For a few slow heartbeats, I held the phone in my hand, waiting for the screen to light up with Ethan's number, but when it didn't happen, acid rose in my throat, threatening to spill the pizza in my stomach onto my crisp white sheets. I wasn't sure why my instincts led my fingers to pull up the contact info for someone I'd only spoken to a few times, but they did. When Tristan had slid his number into my phone on the drive back to his hotel, he said it was only a precaution, and I hadn't dialed it since, but he was someone I knew could help me—or at least I hoped he could.

Swallowing back my hesitation, I clicked on his contact information and typed a message. "Hey, it's Caroline. I think I need your help."

CHAPTER 8

The Phantom

The shrill vibration of my phone on the nightstand jolted me awake, slicing through the thick darkness that enveloped my bedroom. I was still in that stage between sleep and wakefulness where my dreams seemed real, so it took me a moment to read the message. To be honest, the name of the sender had me rubbing my eyes and wondering if I was indeed dreaming.

After a moment, my brain caught up with my squinting eyes and I grabbed my glasses off the side table, my heart rate picking up. It was 12:47 AM, and a message from Ethan's sister at such an ungodly hour could only mean trouble.

"Hey, it's Caroline. I think I need your help," was all the message said.

Her words sent a shiver down my spine as a cold sensation of dread settled in my chest. Although I'd given Caroline my private cellphone number when I was in Alabama, I never expected her to call.

Heart dropping into my stomach, I pushed myself up in the bed and sent a quick reply. "Is everything okay? Did something happen?"

For the next few moments, I watched the three dots on the screen as she appeared to type, hesitate, and then type again. When her message finally came through, a weight dropped in my stomach. "I think I'm being watched."

Cursing under my breath, I kicked my blankets off and dropped my feet to the cold wooden floor, replying to her message. "Did you say anything to Ethan yet?"

By the time I pulled my duffle bag out of the closet and stuffed it with clothes, she still hadn't responded, making me wonder if she regretted her decision to message me at all. The urgency of the situation stripped away any lingering drowsiness as I grabbed Houdini and put him into his carrier, my mind racing with possible scenarios. I couldn't fathom why she would reach out to me instead of her brother, but if she was concerned enough to do so, I had to take it seriously.

When she finally did send a reply, I was already loading my car. "I called, but they didn't answer their phones. Look, I'm probably just being paranoid, and with the baby on the way, I didn't want to worry him if it was nothing, but they didn't answer, so now I'm even more worried."

Heart still in my stomach, I pulled out of the parking garage with my equipment and cat in tow. I couldn't leave him at home, not if I didn't know how long I would be. Already behind the wheel, I couldn't send a return text. Instead, I tried Ethan's number, but he didn't answer. The moment I ended that call, I called Caroline, the sound of rustling meeting my ear before her voice did.

"H-Hello. Tristan?"

The fear in her voice broke my heart. I hated that she was dealing with so much. "I'm on my way there. Why do you think you're being watched?"

She cleared her throat. "There's been a black SUV on the street outside my house for the past few nights. I just thought... I just thought that you could maybe look into it. And maybe you can check Ethan's security system and make sure they're safely at home?"

Even knowing she couldn't see, I shook my head. "We aren't finished hooking everything up, but Ethan's security system isn't hackable—even for me."

I knew my response wasn't what she wanted to hear, but it was the truth. When Ethan's security system was completely set up, I would have a backdoor into it, but only because he trusted me to oversee its operation. He trusted me with his family's safety, which I knew wasn't easy for him.

Caroline blew out a breath, her voice dropping. "Oh. Okay. Well, maybe I could—" A slight break in the connection told me she was receiving another call, which lessened the tension inside my chest—if only a little. "It's Ethan. Thank goodness. Hang on, Tristan. I'll be right back."

For several minutes, the line went silent, leaving me with my thoughts. I debated turning around and heading back home, but with some of the security equipment already having been delivered, and with all my stuff already in the car that was traveling down the freeway at eighty-five miles per hour, I figured I was pretty much committed to keep going.

When Caroline returned to the line, her tone was audibly calmer. "I'm so sorry to bother you, Tristan. I guess I should have known my brother was probably busy, um.. .getting busy."

The awkwardness within her statement made me chuckle. I wanted to respond *lucky him*, because it had been a while since I'd gotten laid, but I figured it would only make the moment more uncomfortable. Instead, I cleared my throat, doing my best to hide the grin in my tone.

"It's really fine, Caroline. I needed to head back soon to finish the work he'd needed me to do anyway. Although..." Pausing, I glanced toward the seat beside me, where glowing eyes stared back at me through the mesh of his carrier. "I'm not sure if Houdini was excited about a road trip."

"Houdini?" The way her voice pitched up made my smile widen. I had to admit, with some of the worry gone, at least the worry of whether Ethan and Scarlett were safe, it was nice to have someone to talk to while I drove. Leaving the city lights behind, the darkness enveloping me was lonely. "Who's Houdini?"

Hearing his name, my black furball meowed. "Oh, uh, Houdini is my cat. I wasn't sure how long I would be gone, and I didn't have anyone to watch him." I shrugged, changing lanes so I could pass an eighteen-wheeler. "I just hope the only hotel in your town allows pets."

Caroline hummed, the sound telling me she was thinking. "I can check for you, but if I'm honest, Evie would absolutely love to play with him, and I have a spare room. There's no need for you to go to a hotel, at least not tonight...especially since I'm the reason you're on the road at three in the morning."

I nearly choked at her unexpected offer. "That's really not necessary. I'm sure I'll find something if they don't allow pet—"

"Nope." She cut me off. "I've already checked, and they don't allow pets. At least for tonight, you're coming here."

For a moment, the line went silent, and I thought she may have changed her mind, which would have been completely fine. She didn't know me and had no reason to open her home to me, but when she spoke again, it sent my heart back into my stomach. "To be honest, Tristan, I don't quite feel safe in my home right now, and I don't want to burden my brother more. Plus, Evie's school is right down the street, so I don't want to pack up and go stay with him." She blew out a breath, and I hated how it rattled. "If you were here, I think I would sleep better, even if it is for only a few days."

After getting Caroline's address and putting it in my navigation system, I only spoke to her for a few minutes longer. To both of our relief, the black SUV was not parked outside on the street, and Ethan had thankfully called her back, undoubtedly offering to go to her house. I didn't see his vehicle in the driveway when I pulled up, but I was glad she'd finally gotten in touch with him.

Although she was adamant about not wanting to burden her brother, I knew that she was not even close to a burden for him. Ethan thrived on taking care of his family. In a way, I believed it was his way of cleaning his soul of all the blood he'd shed. There wasn't one part of him that found annoyance in being there for Caroline and Evie. He didn't need to say it out loud for me to know it was true.

Just like the time before, it took two hours for me to arrive at the small mountain town Caroline and her family called home. The street she lived on was only about three miles away from the bookstore. It was a low-traffic street, just like in the rest of the town, with only a few cottages spread out on either side of the road. Both sides of the street were lined with trees, the area around each house cleared to allow a small yard. Caroline's cottage was more than midway down the street on the left.

Pulling in beside her car, I sent her a text, letting her know I was there. The last thing I wanted to do was wake Evie by knocking on the door.

Once the message was sent, I slipped my phone into my pocket and climbed out of my car, inhaling deeply. Something about the smell of pine, mixed with everything else that grew in the dense forests, had a way of transporting me somewhere else altogether. I may have only been a couple hundred miles from Atlanta, but I felt like I was a world away.

Before unpacking my car of my cat and both of our belongings, I scanned the street, but all was asleep, and there was no black SUV in sight. If it had been there earlier, it was now gone, but I hoped they would return while I was there, so I could get a better idea of what they were doing there. Caroline shouldn't feel fear in her own home, and although I wasn't as intimidating as her brother, I would make damn sure she was safe.

CHAPTER 9

The Phoenix

The moment I stepped onto my front porch and saw Tristan's very tall silhouette standing there with a cat carrier in one hand, several bags over his shoulder, and a litter box on the porch by his feet, my heart skipped a beat. A crooked smile lifted the corner of his mouth, and I couldn't help but smile back. I'd almost forgotten how damn attractive he was, in such a disarming way that it scared me.

"Hey," I said, stepping aside to let him pass. Once he was inside, I moved around him and picked up the litter box, carrying it inside and shutting the door. "I'll set this in the laundry room. Do you think he'll find it?"

Having never owned a cat, I admittedly knew nothing about caring for one.

Before I had a chance to walk away, he set the carrier on the ground and took the box from me, his massive hands grazing mine and sending a shiver through me. I realized at that moment that I was seriously in trouble, and that I was pathetic to allow a chaste touch over a litter box to give me such a reaction. I realized maybe I'd subconsciously offered him a place to stay for reasons beyond just being nice, not that I intended to act on it whatever that other reason could be. I wasn't looking for romance.

The weight of the litter box left my hands as he took it from me, his hazel eyes making me melt. His cat meowed from within the carrier, breaking the hold his gaze had on mine.

"Oh! Should I let him out?" Setting the box beside the carrier, Tristan kneeled, reaching for the zipper. Just inside, a black cat with green eyes peeked through the mesh, patiently waiting to be set free. I kneeled beside Tristan, our shoulders brushing. "He's probably ready to be free after the long drive," he said, unzipping the mesh door, but before he'd even opened it all the way, the cat darted out, slipping beneath the sofa.

Tristan chuckled. "Well, I'm sure he'll come out eventually."

For a moment, we both remained kneeling on the ground, staring at the space beneath the sofa where Houdini had disappeared. The silence between us stretched, but I didn't know what to say.

I was relieved when Tristan broke it, standing and offering me his hand. I took it without question, ignoring how good his skin felt against mine as he pulled me up. When my legs were straight—albeit weak—beneath me, he picked the litter box back up and turned an expectant glance toward me. "Lead the way."

Once the cat's box, food, and water were set up, I showed Tristan to the small guest room, telling him goodnight before going back into my bedroom where Evie was still asleep on the bed. I should've gone to sleep, but the minute he was out of my sight, I didn't know what to do with myself. I was exhausted, having not slept but maybe an hour, but adrenaline surged beneath my skin, making it impossible to settle down.

Climbing in bed beside Evie, I rolled onto my side and grabbed my phone. I didn't know what I was waiting for—why my eyes were still open—but I stared at the screen for a while, listening to Evie's gentle breaths beside me. After about thirty minutes, the screen illuminated in my hand, Tristan's name flashing across the screen and sending the butterflies in my belly into flight. It was ridiculous how this man was affecting me. He was too young for me, and I still mourned for my late husband, but I couldn't deny the loneliness that plagued me, nor could I deny how kind he'd been to my daughter. So, if I could allow the excitement of innocent flirtation to distract me even for a moment, I made the conscious decision to let it happen.

Pulling my bottom lip between my teeth, I unlocked the screen, a smile spreading across my lips as I read his message.

All it said was "thank you," followed by a smile emoji, and all I replied was "you're welcome," but I finished the response with a wink, letting the chips fall where they may.

Sunlight streamed in through sheer curtains, illuminating spiraling specks of dust in the air. The light in my bedroom was still on, reminding me of the extent I'd gone through the night before to ensure no one was in my house. Even after Tristan had arrived and gone to sleep, I'd never turned it off. Even with protection in the other room, I'd barely slept, every creak and whisper of the night wind sending me into a silent panic. Evie lay beside me, her chest rising and falling in the steady rhythm of innocent sleep. As I watched her, the ghost of my nocturnal terror began to dissipate, like mist under the scrutiny of the morning sun.

Was it truly some dead mobster's shadow looming over us? Or had Ethan's warning, meant to protect, inadvertently spawned a monster from my own fears?

My stomach turned as I realized what I'd done, calling a man I barely knew and making him drive all the way to Alabama so I could feel safe in my own home. The air felt heavy with my regret. I had overreacted, letting paranoia get the better of me. I barely knew the guy and now he probably thought I was insane after I'd dragged him into my hysteria.

It only took a second for heat to flood my cheeks as mortification set in and for me to reach for my phone, checking to see if Tristan had messaged me from the other room, but my messages were empty aside from one from my brother checking on me, which I responded to quickly. I gently stroked Evie's back, trying to assure her as much as myself. Although my fingers itched to text him an apology, I couldn't bring myself to revisit my foolishness through text. I would have no choice but to face him when I left my bedroom and hope he didn't look at me as though I had three heads.

Blowing out a breath, I unwrapped myself from the protective cocoon I had formed around Evie and rose unsteadily to my feet. My muscles ached from the tension, but more than that, my heart ached with the realization that the fortress I had built around my daughter was as much a prison as it was a shield.

"Mommy?" Voice groggy from sleep, Evie's eyes blinked open, adjusting to the light.

"Good morning, nugget." I forced a smile, though my cheeks felt heavy, exhaustion weighing them down. "Let's get some breakfast, okay? Oh, before we go into the kitchen, Mr. Tristan is here to help Uncle Ethan and he's in the other room asleep. He brought his cat."

Eyes lighting up like Christmas morning, my daughter jumped out of bed, darting out of the bedroom before I could stop her. A second later, I heard Tristan's voice. He was awake, so it was time to face him and hope he understood.

Pulling on a pair of tights and a long shirt, I twisted my messy hair up into a bun and walked out of my bedroom, following the sound of Evie's endless chatter to the kitchen. My steps slowed as I stepped through the open doorway, a smile spreading across my face as I took in the scene.

Sprawled on the floor beneath the table, Houdini's black tail flicked lazily as Evie petted the top of his head, a big smile across her face. Standing by the stove in a pair of gray joggers and a plain white tee shirt, Tristan moved something around in a pan.

The moment he saw me, a bashful smile tugged up the side of his mouth and he slid a cup of coffee across the counter to me. "Mommy! Mommy!" Eve shrieked, jumping up from the floor to hug my leg. "Mr. Tristan is making pancakes!'

When I looked back up at him, my eyebrow arching, I found him smiling back at me, his hazel eyes near golden in the sunlight streaming in through the curtains. "Is that so?"

Grabbing my hands, Evie tugged me around the table to the stove, where pancakes were indeed browning in the pan. "Yes, Mommy! He is a super spy, too, because he knew I wanted pancakes. I didn't even have to tell him!"

"Hrmm." Pursing my lips, I looked back at him as he flipped the pancake. "That could be a dangerous power to have—being able to read minds." He held my gaze for a moment, and I really hoped he wasn't reading my mind, because all my mind was telling me to do was to kiss him for making my daughter's morning joyful—for driving all the way to Alabama to make sure we were safe—for being so damned good looking. I was starting to think I didn't need to have a reason at all.

His smile twisted into a smirk at my comment, but he looked away from me to scoop the pancakes onto a plate. "I guess it could be dangerous," he said, shrugging one shoulder and handing the first plate to Evie. "But it could be a good thing, allowing me to know exactly what someone wants and needs, so I can give them just that."

I may have stopped breathing at the innuendo, or maybe my breath just got stuck for a moment, but all I could do was stare at him like a deer in the headlights, even as he held a plate of pancakes out to me.

After an awkward second of me not grabbing the plate, his smile returned, lighting up his eyes with more than a little mischief in them. "So, do you want something other than pancakes, Caroline? Your wish is my command."

"Huh? Oh," I choked out, nearly dropping the plate when I reached out to take it. "Pancakes are great. Tha-thank you. I love pancakes."

I was smooth. Really smooth. The smoothest, but I couldn't convince my cheeks that flushed with complete mortification for the second time that morning as I walked away and set my plate on the table, hoping he couldn't see how he affected me. There was a particularly good chance that he hadn't been flirting with me at all, and that I'd read the signals and interpreted his words all wrong, but I hoped that wasn't the case. If it was, I had a feeling I would be experiencing plenty more embarrassing moments over the next few days, and by the time he left to return to Atlanta, he would absolutely be looking at me like I'd grown two additional heads.

CHAPTER 10

The Phantom

The morning sun was a gentle intruder, its rays filtering through the curtains until I could no longer feign sleep. I stretched as much as I could on the bed that was made for people much shorter than my six-foot-four-inch frame, every muscle fiber lengthening and contracting. My eyes fluttered open, the room coming into focus—the quaint charm of Caroline's cottage bringing a sleepy smile to my face. The scent of aged wood mingled with the faintest hint of lavender, and I took a moment to let it ground me.

A sense of contentment washed over me, something I hadn't felt in so long that it was almost foreign. It was strange to think that after years of hiding behind my hacker alias, I could finally just be Tristan again, at least while I was there. The thought sent a shiver down my spine, and I couldn't help but wonder if this newfound peace would last. Lying in bed, I thought about Caroline—her protectiveness toward her daughter and how she persevered even while grieving the loss of her husband. This woman and her daughter had already touched something deep inside me that I didn't know existed. I was going soft, but I didn't think it was a bad thing.

The tranquility of the cottage seemed to seep into my bones, healing some of the wounds I'd accumulated during my time as Phantom, and even before. It allowed me to let my guard down, if only for a moment, and bask in the serenity of a normal life.

"Mommy said you brought a kitty!" The pitter patter of little feet pulled me away from my pancake batter when Evie ran into the kitchen, throwing herself onto the floor beside Houdini. The sight of her hairless head sent my heart into my stomach, but the joy in her eyes when she crawled under the table to pet my cat made me grin. If she was sick, I couldn't tell.

Crossing the small kitchen, I crouched beside her, scratching Houdini behind the ear. "I did. His name is Houdini."

Houdini's tail flicked like he didn't have a care in the world as Evie leaned forward and kissed him on the head. "Hi, Houdini."

Remembering I had pancake batter sitting on the counter, I stood, heading back to the stove where the skillet was already hot. The pancakes were from an instant mix I'd found in the pantry, but I figured it would do in a pinch. "Can you look after him while I cook breakfast?"

She responded with a giggled "Yes" as she flopped like a fish on the floor beneath the table next to my only partially amused feline friend.

Having never been around children, or at least not since I'd adopted him, I would have expected him to be less at ease around a hyper little kid, but he lay there cool as a cucumber, tail flicking as he nuzzled into her hand. "See? He likes you already."

Taking a sip of my coffee, I couldn't help but grin at their instant connection.

As I was watching Evie and Houdini on the floor, leaning near the stove to make sure not to burn the pancakes, the sound of footsteps caught my attention, and I looked up just in time to see Caroline entering the kitchen from the open doorway and bending over to give Evie a kiss. She wore black tights and an oversized T-shirt with her dark curls pulled up into a bun. Despite her casual attire, she radiated an undeniable beauty that left me momentarily breathless, and the way the tights hugged her perfectly rounded ass left me with a semi.

I grinned up at her, turning around to pour her a cup of coffee and willing my cock to behave when her child was in the room.

When I turned back around, I slid the mug of coffee across the counter to her, her light blue eyes never leaving mine as she reached out to grab it.

"Mommy! Mommy!" Jumping up from the floor, Evie wrapped her arms around Caroline's leg. The way they looked at each other was pure love—joyous and unconditional. "Mr. Tristan is making pancakes!"

Eyebrow arching, Caroline looked at me, the playful expression on her face making me grin wider. "Is that so? " she asked, but before I could respond, Evie grabbed both Caroline's hands, dragging her toward me. I watched them, curious what they would do next. "Yes, Mommy! He's a super spy too, because he knew I wanted pancakes. I didn't even have to tell him!"

I wasn't sure where Evie had gotten the idea that I was a super spy, but it was fucking adorable, so I played along.

Pursing her lips, Caroline looked back at me just as I was flipping a pancake. "That could be a dangerous power to have—being able to read minds."

Although she was answering Evie's statement, the way she was looking at me told me she was directing the response at me. I may have been an enamored idiot who was developing a crush on the sister of the most dangerous man I knew, but something in her eyes told me she was flirting with me—or maybe it was my undersexed and over-ly-horny mind reading into the innocent facial gestures of this absolutely stunning woman. Either way, two could play.

Lips twisting into a smirk, I turned my eyes away and plated the pancakes. "I guess it could be dangerous?" Shrugging, I handed the first plate of pancakes to Evie, who darted back to the table, dropping to the ground to sit beside Houdini again—plate and all.

"But it could be a good thing...knowing exactly what someone wants and needs, so I can give them just that."

When Caroline's jaw went slack and she just stared at me, not taking the plate of food I was holding out for her, I knew the innuendo in my answer had been received, although I wasn't sure what she thought about the shameless way I was trying to flirt with her. I had admittedly been out of the game for a while.

After a few silent moments, where I almost heard the crickets myself, I smiled, a surge of mischief surging through my veins. "So, do you want something other than pancakes, Caroline? Your wish is my command."

A cherry-red flush crept up Caroline's exposed upper chest all the way to her cheeks as she took the plate of pancakes from my hand. "Huh? Oh. Pancakes are great. Tha-thank you. I love pancakes." Taking one more flushed look at me, she scurried to the table, leaving me feeling victorious. She *absolutely* knew I was flirting with her, and I'd meant every word. If this woman wanted anything within my power to give, I would tear through the world to give it to her. After everything she'd been through, she deserved it, and I didn't know how Ethan would feel about it, but I really wanted to get to know his sister better.

Plating the last of the pancakes, I joined her at the table, sitting in the chair directly across from her. With the flush still coloring her cheeks, she wasted no time digging in.

"Tristan, these pancakes are amazing," she said between bites, her blue eyes bright in the sunlight coming in through the window. It would have been so easy to get lost in them, but I looked away, taking a bite of my own food.

"Thank you. It's been a while since I've cooked for anyone other than myself." I huffed a chuckle, still unsure what possessed me to cook at all. "I don't even cook for myself that much. When you're always alone, it's just easier to order out."

Her eyebrow lifted at my admission, but she didn't ask me about why I was always alone—thankfully. It was totally by choice, and most of the time I liked it that way, but I didn't have anyone like her in Atlanta. "Maybe you should consider opening a cafe when you're not busy hacking into the world's most secure databases," she teased, her smirk making my core heat.

"Phantom's Pancakes?" I suggested playfully.

She scrunched her nose but then giggled just a little. "I dunno. Maybe you could use your super spy powers to give people *whatever* they want."

Cock turning hard almost instantly, I was glad Evie had moved from beneath the table and was standing at the kitchen counter where Houdini had jumped onto the windowsill. I held Caroline's stare, taking a sip of my coffee. "Nah. I'd rather use my special powers on truly special people."

Caroline's eyes lit up with mirth as she faked a laugh. "Well, Scarlett and Ethan are tied up at their store today, so how about a little adventure with Evie and me?"

The side of my lips lifted in a grin. "An adventure sounds perfect."

As we walked down the leaf-littered sidewalk of downtown toward the park, Evie skipped ahead, her jubilant spirit seemingly unscarred by everything she'd gone through. Caroline and I fell into steps beside each other, the floral scent of her shampoo nearly making my eyes roll back in my head. There was something about that damn floral shampoo that turned me on, or maybe it was just her. To be honest, it was all her. Either way, being beside her tethered me to the moment, and there was nowhere I would have rather been.

"Mr. Tristan, are you good at pushing swings?" Evie's question grabbed my attention, her bright eyes fixed on mine as they waited for a response.

"I guess we'll find out." My conspiratorial wink earned a giggle before Evie turned back around and continued to skip toward the playground.

"Thank you for this," I murmured, unsure if I was thanking her for the invitation or something deeper—perhaps the chance to be a part of something resembling normalcy.

Her hand brushed against mine as she turned up to flash me one of those stunning smiles, sending a zing of electricity through me. For a moment, I wondered what she would have thought if I held her hand. I'd only just met her, but still I wanted to.

"Thank you for being here," she replied, reaching out to help Evie open the gate to the park. "I was probably overreacting last night, but I still appreciate you not doubting me even when I was doubting myself."

The park was alive with the vibrant colors of spring, flowers blooming and filling the well-manicured play area with color. Evie's laughter filled the air like a melody, her small figure darting toward the swings with an infectious excitement that brought a smile to my lips. I followed her, standing behind her to push her swing once she climbed on.

"Higher, Super Spy Tristan!" she squealed as I pushed her forward, each soaring arc of the swing accompanied by her gleeful laughter. She kicked her legs with wild abandon, propelling herself toward the sky, and for a moment I found myself envying her unfettered spirit. Even with all she'd suffered, she'd somehow been able to just let it all go, or at least she was exceptionally good at compartmentalizing. I only wished I could be so good at pushing things to the back of my mind.

Caroline stood nearby, the smile on her face telling me how much it meant to her to see Evie on the mend, but I never missed the emotions that shadowed her eyes—those she refused to let come to the surface.

"Let's go slide!" Before the swing even slowed to a stop, Evie was off, darting toward the slide several feet away. We followed behind, watching as she climbed the steps and slid down, giggling the entire way.

"Your turn, Super Spy Tristan," Caroline teased, bumping me with her shoulder.

I hesitated for only a moment, wondering if I was too big to even attempt such a thing, but when I looked at Evie's expectant face, something within me shifted. It wasn't just about letting go, it was about embracing the here and now, about being part of a memory that would be cherished long after the day faded.

So, too big or not, I climbed the steps, taking a few at a time with my tall stature. When I reached the top, I paused, looked down at the slide that seemed a lot taller than it appeared from the ground. But then, Evie's excited cheers and Caroline's encouraging smile spurred me on, and I released my grip on control, allowing gravity to take over.

The wind rushed past me, a fleeting escape from reality, and for those few seconds, I was free—free from the ghosts of my past, free from the chains of my isolation. When I landed with a thud, their laughter enveloped me, reminding me that joy could be found in the simplest of actions, especially when you had others to share those moments with.

"Again! Again!" Evie chanted. So, we went again and again. All three of us.

The sun was descending behind the mountains as we made our way back to Caroline's cottage later that afternoon. My heart felt lighter than it had in years, the warmth of the afternoon's laughter still lingering in my chest as we stepped inside.

"Do you want to play a game, Mr. Tristan?" Evie stared up at me, her eyes shining with anticipation. Even after a long day, she was still full of energy.

"Sounds like a perfect plan," I replied, allowing her to lead me toward the shelf where an array of colorful boxes awaited us.

Ultimately, she settled on Monopoly, although Caroline and I both knew the game took no less than days to play. When the time came, I intended to volunteer myself to accidentally bump into the table and knock the board over.

"Who will you be, Mr. Tristan?" Evie asked, holding out the tiny metal figurines for me to choose from.

"Ah, the car." Taking the tiny metal car from her, I placed it on the board. "Reminds me of my first classic car, a beat-up old thing but it kept me moving."

"Nice choice," Caroline chimed in, her grin mischievous as she claimed the thimble. "Be prepared to lose, though. I'm a Monopoly master."

"Is that a challenge?" I raised an eyebrow, a competitive spark igniting within me. It was a side of myself I hadn't shown in quite some time—a side I'd almost forgotten existed.

"Bring it on, *Phantom.*"

CHAPTER II
The Phoenix

K neeling beside the tub, my fingers worked gently across Evie's scalp, loving the sight of new growth. Bubbles rose and popped around her as she played with a baby doll in the water.

"I liked it when Mr. Tristan ended up in jail and couldn't get out." She giggled, still giddy after kicking both Tristan and my butt at Monopoly.

"You put us both in there, nugget. You've gotten very good at counting money." Leaning her head back, she giggled harder. These moments were precious, islands of normalcy in a sea of uncertainty—a sea we'd been navigating ever since Daniel left us.

"Can we play again tomorrow?" Big blue eyes looked up at me, making it nearly impossible to say no. "I like Mr. Tristan. He's nice isn't he, Mommy?"

I leaned forward and kissed her on the nose. "He is, and if he isn't too busy helping Uncle Ethan, we'll see if he can spare some time for the world's cutest jailer."

"Good." She nodded as though that was that, splashing a little more before settling down.

Scooping up more water, I poured it over her head, careful not to get any soap in those bright, curious eyes—eyes that mirrored Daniel's in a way that both warmed and shattered my heart.

"Mommy?" she asked, her tone turning pensive.

"Yes, nugget?"

"Will I have hair like yours again? Long and pretty?"

"Absolutely." My throat tightened just a bit, hating that such things were on her mind. "Your hair will grow back thick and beautiful, just like Rapunzel's."

"Then I can use it to rescue Mr. Tristan from jail!" Her laughter filled the room once more, echoing off the tiles and drowning out the melancholic whispers of loss that lingered at the edges of my thoughts.

With the last of the bubbles disappearing down the drain, I dried and dressed Evie and tucked her into bed. Alone in the quiet aftermath, I braced my hands on the counter, willing my heart to stay anchored in the present, but memories were unruly creatures. They didn't heed such commands. After spending the entire day with Tristan, a day I'd enjoyed more than even I wanted to admit, I still couldn't force down that ache that stirred in my chest. Three years had passed since the accident claimed my husband's life, yet the grief clung to me like a second skin. I just wondered what it would take to move on. Not forget...just move on.

"It's nice outside. Do you want to sit with me?" Tristan's voice, a soft baritone infused with warmth, pulled me from my downward spiral as he passed down the hall from the guest room. I steadied my breath, pushing myself to smooth out my features and leave the bathroom.

"Sounds perfect," I replied, my voice betraying none of the conflicting swirl of emotions.

Taking one more peek into Evie's room, I gently pulled the door closed behind me, a quiet click echoing in my ears. The house seemed to hold its breath, waiting for what came next. The soft glow of moonlight filtered through the windows, the light guiding me toward the back patio where I knew Tristan would be waiting.

When I stepped outside, he was sitting in one of the wooden chairs, two glasses of wine shimmering on the table beside him.

"She's asleep," I said as I sat beside him, reaching out to take one of the glasses. The night sky stretched above us like an infinite canvas, painted with countless constellations that glittered amidst a sea of darkness.

"Your daughter is remarkable," he said, the admiration clear in his tone. "She reminds me so much of you."

His words warmed my chest, a wistful smile tugging at my lips as I gazed up at the stars. "Thank you, but she's so much stronger than me. Her strength amazes me every day. I can only hope that I'm able to give her the love and support she needs."

"You are," he said, his eyes meeting mine, somehow cutting straight into my soul. "You're everything she could ever ask for and more, Caroline. Never doubt that."

His words stirred a swell of emotion within me, bringing tears to my eyes. If only he knew how *much* I doubted myself—how weak I sometimes felt, as though the pain was too much. But I continued to fight for my daughter.

My heart clenched at the thought of the losses we had endured and the pain that had woven itself into the fabric of our lives. But in that moment, as Tristan's gaze held mine with unwavering certainty, I felt a sense of connection that transcended the darkness. Maybe if he believed in me, and Evie believed in me, I could learn to believe in myself too...just maybe.

"Thank you," I whispered, allowing myself to lean into the comfort and understanding he offered so freely. "I appreciate that. It's easy to doubt yourself when the stakes are always so high."

Expression softening, Tristan's hand reached toward mine on the armrest between our chairs, resting on top of it. For a moment, the touch was surprising, and I wasn't sure if it was something I was ready for, but his skin against mine sent such a wave of awareness through my body, making it impossible to pull my hand away. It felt too good.

As though he could sense my insecurity, the corner of his mouth tipped up in a grin. "If a Superwoman like you doubts herself, what does that say for the rest of us super-heroes?"

Midway through taking a sip of my wine, I nearly choked and spit it out. Although he tried to be smooth, he was just as awkward as I was. "Last I checked, Phantom, you were a super *spy*, not a superhero."

"Hey. That's just semantics." He leaned back, eyes widening in mock offense. "I, too, am a superhero. Ask your brother—or even Houdini. Ask Houdini."

I laughed again, taking another sip of my wine, savoring the rich flavor that danced on my tongue. It was a good bottle of red, one I'd been saving to share. As I lowered the glass, our eyes met, and something in my chest opened.

"Isn't it amazing?" I mused, my gaze drifting back to the stars above, not ready to analyze how this man was already burrowing into my heart as easily as he found his way into firewalled security systems. "How vast the universe is, and how insignificant our problems can feel when we look up at the night sky?"

"It's humbling." With his hand still holding mine, Tristan looked up at the sky, adjusting his glasses. "Although they're nearly impossible to see in the city, whenever I feel overwhelmed, I like to get into my car and drive far enough out of the city to see the stars. Stargazing has a way of reminding me that there's always something bigger than us, that maybe I need to look at things from a different angle or move on from something that isn't benefiting me. It just helps to keep things in perspective."

"Which constellation is your favorite?" I asked, intrigued by this glimpse into his passions.

"Orion," he replied without hesitation. "I used to imagine myself as a hunter, navigating through the darkness with only the stars to guide me."

"Ah, so you're a dreamer too," I teased, enjoying the way it made me feel. A little harmless flirting wouldn't hurt anyone.

"Guilty," he confessed with a devastatingly handsome grin. "What about you? Do you have a favorite constellation?"

"Definitely Cassiopeia." Holding my hand up in front of me, I traced the distinctive W shape with my finger across the sparkling tapestry of space. "She may be a queen, but she's also a symbol of resilience and strength. I've always admired those qualities." They were the qualities I saw in my daughter.

Tristan's hand squeezed mine gently, his eyes turning to meet mine again. "Sounds like this stunningly amazing woman I know."

"Perhaps," I conceded, allowing myself a small smile before taking another sip of my wine. My heart fluttered at his words, but I didn't dare let my guard down completely. Not yet.

"I can only imagine how difficult these past few years have been for you. Losing Daniel, raising Evie on your own and her illness…"

"It hasn't been easy," I admitted, swallowing the lump in my throat. "But I've learned my best to cope, to adapt, to find strength in the face of adversity…or at least I do my best to. It's what Daniel would have wanted for us—for me to carry on, to keep living, even when it feels like the world has crumbled beneath my feet."

"Your resilience is inspiring," Tristan said, his eyes never leaving mine. "You've faced unimaginable challenges and still managed to create a safe, loving home for your daughter. And you help her to live as normal a life as she can, considering what she's suffering through. Even with her own struggles, she's smart and joyful. That's all because of you, and that's truly remarkable."

For a moment, I just allowed his words to soak in, filling all the dark places where my doubts went to hide and fester, my hand still cradled inside his. His words had touched me so much deeper than he realized, and as he gazed into my eyes, glancing a moment down to my lips and then back up, all I wanted to do was kiss him, but I suppressed the urge. I wasn't sure if I was ready for that yet. Instead, I smiled, the gesture genuine. "Thank you, Tristan. That means a lot to me."

We lingered there for a moment longer, a palpable tension building between us, fueled by an undeniable chemistry, and uncertainty of what would happen next. But it was too soon to move forward, or at least that was how I felt at that moment, and I knew we both needed rest.

"I'm going to head to bed," I said, standing from my chair and reaching for the doorknob.

Although I expected him to remain where he was, he stood as well, taking a step toward me. "I'll do the same. If I know your brother, he has a full day of work planned for me tomorrow."

I smiled and nodded, knowing it was true. "Okay, well... Goodnight, Tristan."

"Goodnight, Caroline," he responded, his hand touching the small of my back as he leaned forward to kiss my cheek.

The moment his lips touched my skin, my eyes fell closed, electricity surging through my body that only made me want to kiss him more. Being around him was really starting to test my willpower, but when he pulled away, I allowed him to.

With one last lingering look, we retreated to our separate rooms, the sound of our footsteps echoing in the quiet cottage. Heart pounding with a blend of anticipation and uncertainty, I closed the door behind me, leaning against it as I tried to catch my breath.

In the solitude of my room, my thoughts swirled around the undeniable connection that I was starting to feel with Tristan, and how to make my conscience okay with it. I didn't know what the future held, but I knew one thing: I really liked Tristan, as did my daughter, and a man like him didn't just fall on your doorstep every day, so maybe it was time for me to try something new.

CHAPTER 12

The Phantom

Waking up the following morning, I rubbed my eyes and rolled over, a smile already on my face. I reached for my glasses that rested on the nightstand next to a framed photograph of Caroline and her late husband, Daniel, with little Evie riding on his shoulders. The image sent an ache through my heart that I couldn't quite decipher. I knew it was partly because I felt empathy for what she and her daughter had gone through, but it was more than that. She was more than just a widow raising a little girl to me.

A knock at the door pulled my attention away from my thoughts. I sat up in the bed, running my hand through my disheveled hair. "Come in."

"Good morning," Caroline's gentle voice greeted me as she entered the room, a tray laden with breakfast goodies in her hands. Her long black hair was down and cascaded over her shoulders, the light blue tank top bringing out the color of her eyes. Even first thing in the morning, she was absolutely beautiful. "I hope you slept well."

"Better than I have in a long time," I admitted, pushing myself up to sit against the headboard, hoping my morning wood wasn't didn't pitch a tent in the blankets where she could see it. Or did I? Forcing my impure thoughts away, I focused on the stunning woman before me. The mere presence of Caroline and her daughter seemed to fill the void in me that had consumed me for far too long, so I wanted to soak it in as much as I could.

Crossing the room, she set the tray down on the side table, steam rising from the mug of coffee, the aroma of freshly baked muffins making my stomach growl. There was even a bowl of cut fruit. She'd gone out of her way to make breakfast for me, which only made me like her more.

"Thank you, Superwoman. This looks amazing."

"Anything for my favorite hacker," she teased, a hint of mischief sparkling in her eyes. I couldn't help but grin back at her, loving the lighthearted banter.

"Favorite? I'm honored." Unable to resist, I bit into one of the muffins, groaning at how good it was. Her eyebrows quirked up at my overdramatization, which only made me grin wider. "What? It's really good. You are a woman of many talents. Superwoman—like I said."

"Tristan!" Evie's voice shattered our moment like a stone through glass, her giggles filling the air as she burst into the room. Still in her pajamas, she bounded toward me with endless energy, her eyes bright as though she hadn't just rolled out of bed. I wished I had that much energy first thing in the morning. I barely had time to set my coffee down on the table before she leaped onto the bed, bouncing the entire mattress.

"Hey there, wild child," I said, unable to suppress a chuckle at her infectious enthusiasm. "What's got you so excited this morning?"

"Mommy says we're going to Uncle Ethan's house today!" she beamed, bouncing on the bed again. "I can't wait!"

Stepping out of the cottage with Caroline and Evie by my side an hour later, I breathed in the crisp mountain air as I led them to my black 1969 Mustang—*my* baby. The car had always been a symbol of my independence, a sleek machine that allowed me to escape when the weight of the world became too heavy.

"Wow, Mr. Tristan!" Evie exclaimed, running forward, her stuffed llama flopping in her hands. "Do we get to ride in your car today? It's a super cool spy car!"

"Thank you, Captain." Smiling back down at her, I pulled the door open. "Are you ready to show me how to get to your Uncle Ethan's house?"

Without hesitation, she nodded, climbing into the back seat, and allowing her mother to strap her into the seat-belt.

"Nice car," Caroline said, her tone playful. "Almost makes me forget about the whole 'lawless computer nerd' thing."

A smile tugged at the corners of my mouth as I watched her strap in Evie, shamelessly checking her out. I found myself doing that a lot lately. "Thanks. I'm glad you approve."

Once everyone was settled, I slid behind the wheel and started the engine. The Mustang roared to life, its power vibrating through me like an extension of my own being. I could have let Caroline drive, but I rarely had the chance to take my car out on mountain roads, so I looked forward to any opportunity to do so. Maybe I could even impress her a little with how I handled the curves.

The roar of the engine bounced off the mountainside as I guided my car up the winding road, its black sheen catching glints of the midday sun. Beside me, Caroline's gaze danced out over the landscape, her fingers tracing imaginary on the fabric of her tights. The sky was an endless expanse of blue, stretching out to touch the peaks of the mountains in the distance. Who would have thought Alabama could be so beautiful?

"Over there," she pointed, "is a trail that leads to a waterfall I've yet to explore. It's supposed to be beautiful this time of year."

The corners of her mouth lifted in a smile that was part longing, part invitation. I glanced at her, the warmth of her enthusiasm disrupting my cool isolation I usually kept draped around myself like a cloak. All I wanted to do was touch her cheek. She was so fucking beautiful, it hurt. "Sounds like it's worth the hike. I haven't been on one in a while."

"Maybe we could go together sometime." A hint of play-fulness threaded through her tone, sending a surge of heat through me. "With Ethan and Scarlett so busy, and not knowing anyone here, I've yet to see much of the area."

"Maybe," I murmured, steering the car around a tight bend, the thought lingering like the sweet aftertaste of forbidden fruit. I was fairly sure Ethan would want to kick my ass if he knew how filthy my thoughts about his sister were turning, but I wasn't sure if I cared. I was still going to think about her when I stroked myself before bed.

"Have you ever been up here before?" she asked, still staring at the passing landscape. "Well, aside from this last time when you came for the day."

"Never. I grew up in the city. I traveled a little, but never here." A pang of regret hit me as I thought about all the years I spent locked away in dark rooms and hidden corners, my world limited to the confines of a computer screen. "It's incredible."

"Well, wait until you see what's coming up." There was a hint of excitement in her voice that made me smile, as though she couldn't wait to show her world off to me. "This next stretch of road has some of the most breathtaking views. It's one of the reasons why Ethan and Scarlett chose this place. They wanted a sanctuary—somewhere they could escape to—when the world became too much."

I could understand the appeal, the allure of a simpler life far removed from the chaos and complexities of our daily existence. And for a moment, I allowed myself to imagine a different future, one where I could trade shadows and secrets for the warmth and comfort of a loving family.

In the backseat, Evie sat quietly, her eyelids already drooping as she fought off a nap. When she caught me glancing at her in the rearview mirror, she sat up straighter. "Mr. Tristan, did you know there are secret places in the mountains where the faeries live? Aunt Scarlett told me about them."

My grin widened, my eyes going wide in excitement to reflect hers as I met her eyes in the mirror again. "Is that so? Well, it certainly looks like a magical place."

She nodded. "Mhmm, Auntie says they're very shy, though. You have to be very quiet, or they'll hide."

From the corner of my eye, I saw Caroline smile, before turning my eyes back to her daughter. "Then we'll have to tread softly, won't we?" The absolute wonder on Evie's face filled my chest with a lightness that was completely alien to me, but completely welcome. I knew I would eventually have to return to my life in Atlanta, but I was already dreading it.

Ethan emerged from the front door as we pulled into the driveway, his presence commanding against the very domestic background of the cabin's porch. Scarlett stood beside him, radiant in a simple ivory dress with her hand resting on her baby bump. After everything she'd been through, seeing her smiling gave me a little more faith in the world.

Stepping off the porch as I parked, Ethan opened the passenger door for his sister, helping Evie out of the car once Caroline was out of the way. "Welcome back, Tristan. Glad you could make it."

"Wouldn't miss it for the world," I replied, grabbing my tech gear out of the trunk. "Anything for my new family."

Caroline's laughter filled the air as she held a mumbled conversation with Scarlett several feet away. Stealing a glance at her, I grinned, imagining what they could be talking about. I didn't doubt it involved why we'd shown up together. Although it was innocent, I could see Scarlett picking on her about it just to get a rise out of her.

Once we went inside, Ethan and I headed into the basement, where Ethan had converted nearly the entire lower level on one side of the house into a safe room apartment. It was their sanctuary within a sanctuary—a place to hide if danger ever found them again. Some would have thought it overkill, but after the things they'd gone through, and the world both Ethan and I knew existed, it wasn't. There was no such thing as being too vigilant when it came to protecting those you loved.

"I told Scarlett what you found out about her old man," Ethan said a few hours later as he stared at the computer screen in the safe room where images blinked to life one by one. "He's like an old wound that never seems to heal for her, even without him being an active part of her life."

Noticing one of the screens remained blacked out, I reached for the control panel to adjust the connection. "Seems so. Delacroix's gang doesn't strike me as the type to let bygones be bygones. Ivy's testimony could put a lot of them away. I'm sure they're going to be desperate to get rid of him before he can."

Ethan grunted, the sound heavy with unspoken fears. For someone who was always so careful and controlled, I knew the uncertainty must keep him up at night. "That's why we're turning this place into Fort Knox. No one's laying a finger on Scarlett or the baby. Even if they don't know my identity, they know hers. I don't want her to feel like she can't live her life or be safe. Her father put her in this predicament, but I have to do everything I can to keep them safe until this case blows over—until they're hopefully locked up."

"We'll get there, boss," I said, sitting in the chair beside him and taking the mouse he'd abandoned. My eyes scanned the monitors, watching as the last of the cameras blinked online, covering every shadowed nook of the property.

As I moved closer to the displays, Ethan rolled his chair back to get out of my way. "What are you working on now?"

My fingers flew across the keyboard, bringing the grid up on the screen. The green dots popped into existence, each one representing an unseen eye. "Syncing the motion sensors. If a leaf falls, we'll know about it."

CHAPTER 13

The Phoenix

"**I** wish Daniel could be here to see this."

Even as I was surrounded by an explosion of pink while helping Scarlett fold the baby clothes she'd just washed, sadness made my chest ache. So much had happened since I'd been in her shoes—so much that left me broken. She looked up at me, endless love and support showing in her brown eyes. "I do too, Cara. If it's too much—"

"No." No matter how much it hurt, the last thing I wanted was for her to feel like she couldn't share her joy with me. I was excited for my new niece's arrival too. It was just that my wounds were always there. I wasn't sure if they would ever heal completely. I forced a smile, my heart swelling with joy for her, but as I reached for another garment from the bag of Evie's old baby clothes I'd given them, my fingers brushed the fabric of Daniel's favorite shirt that had somehow ended up in the bag, one I'd never quite been able to part with, just like the wedding band around my finger. The texture against my skin was a bittersweet pang, a ghost of his presence that lingered in threads and memories.

"Caroline?" Scarlett's voice pulled me from the depths of my thoughts, her dark eyes searching mine with concern.

"Sorry, I'm just—" Pausing, I swallowed the lump in my throat. "I'm really happy for you, Scarlett. Truly."

"Hey," she said softly, reaching across the pile of laundry to squeeze my hand. "He'd be so proud of you, you know? Of how strong you've been for Evie."

I nodded, unable to speak past the tightness in my chest. "It's just that..." Setting the blanket I folded into the open drawer, I shook my head. "It's just that I don't think he would believe Ethan is married and expecting a baby. He would be so proud."

I'd meant every word, and Scarlett knew it. Her eyes danced as she laughed. "To be honest, I wouldn't have believed it seven months ago, but he's proven to be pretty amazing."

Her words warmed a little piece of me that had grown cold. The smile that spread across my lips this time was genuine. "He always has been. I'm just glad he finally showed that part of himself to someone other than me and Evie."

"Mommy, look!" Evie's cheerful voice pulled my attention to the doorway, where she stood holding a picture she must have just drawn of a stick figure baby holding hands with a stick figure little girl wearing a pink dress in the shape of a triangle, both hairless. "This is me and baby Adelaide!"

Not waiting for an invitation, she darted into the room, doing her best to prop the drawing up against the golden lamp on the dresser.

"That's beautiful, nugget. Did you draw it all by yourself?"

Her smile grew as she nodded vigorously, her missing front tooth making her even cuter. "I did! She's going to be my best friend, so I wanted to draw some pictures for her and give her some of my toys."

"That's such a nice idea," Scarlett said, crossing the room and leaning over the dresser to take a closer look at the picture.

Filled with pride at herself, Evie rocked back and forth on the balls of her feet, which was the first time I noticed she was wearing a pair of Scarlett's heels that were many sizes too big for her.

Covering my mouth to hide my giggle, I stepped forward as well, patting her on the back. "Those are some nice shoes you're wearing too, Evie. Where did you find those?"

Even though she was having a tough time staying balanced, she straightened her spine. "These are *auntie* shoes, and since I'm going to be an auntie, I needed some too—just like Auntie Scarlett."

Holding back what I knew would be a fit of giggles, Scarlett and I looked at each other, both of our smiles wide. I was about to respond and tell Evie that I would have to buy a pair of *auntie* shoes in her size, but she'd already moved on to the next thing, feet clacking against the hardwood floor as she headed back down the hall toward her room.

With all the laundry put away, Scarlett and I headed into the kitchen. It was only four in the afternoon, but we were both hungry, and with Ethan and Tristan having worked both inside and outside for hours, we figured they were too.

"Chop vegetables or stir fry?" Scarlett asked, already handing me the knife. We'd been cooking together long enough that we already knew our jobs when we did. We enjoyed doing things together—just like sisters. With me chopping and her cooking, we fell into an easy rhythm.

"So..." The words hung on my tongue long enough that Scarlett's eyes flicked up to me, an expectant look in them. "Um, so tell me a little about Tristan. Do you know him well?"

When the corner of her mouth curled up, I realized I was not hiding my reason for asking as well as I had thought, and I was slightly mortified. "Why do you ask?"

I rolled my eyes and shoulder-bumped her, making her laugh. "No particular reason. I mean, Ethan trusts him, so he's a good guy, right?"

Turning her gaze back to mine, she wiggled her eyebrows, sending a flush of heat across my face.

I bumped into her again but laughed. "So, he's cute. Sue me for noticing."

Grinning from ear to ear, Scarlett bumped me back, making me drop the tomato in the sink. "Hey, you. Watch it."

She shook her head, but her smile told me I was never going to hear the end of this conversation. "You know I'm not fussing you, Cara. Yes, your brother does trust Tristan, so that tells me that he's a good guy." When her eyes flicked up to meet mine again, there was something deeply genuine in them that set me a little more at ease. "You've gone without for a long time, Cara. I fully support your quest to find love again. But hey if all you're trying to do is get laid... Well, I support you doing that too."

"Who's getting laid?" I nearly hit the floor when Tristan's voice interrupted our conversation.

More embarrassed than I'd ever been in my entire life, I looked up to find his tall frame leaning against the door frame, a mischievous smirk on his face.

"Well, you see—"

Before Scarlett could finish her statement, I bumped her with my shoulder again. One of us was definitely going to end up with a bruise.

"No one is getting laid," I said, my voice a little higher pitched than I'd intended.

Tristan's eyebrows shot up, his hands sliding into his pockets as he chuckled.

"Speak for yourself," Scarlett said, stirring the chicken in the pan. "I'm definitely getting laid."

Unable to handle the intense embarrassment that was turning me the color of a firetruck, I threw my head back and groaned. "You guys are insufferable."

Tristan chuckled again as he crossed the room to grab a bottle of water. "It smells great in here. Are we eating soon?"

Scarlett shrugged. "You'll have to ask Caroline, because she said—"

Breath or not, I pressed my hand across Scarlett's mouth, the next embarrassing line silenced, but then they both started laughing.

So, when my brother walked in a moment later, he walked in to see both Scarlett and Tristan laughing at me, and me red as a crawfish, holding my hand over Scarlett's mouth. No wonder his face was a mask of confusion, but it didn't take him long to laugh at me too.

Once the teasing died down, we all sat at the dining room table to eat, but every time I glanced up at Tristan, I found him looking at me. It was as though he had something he wanted to say, but wasn't ready yet, or maybe he didn't want to say it in front of the others.

"Caroline, Scarlett, there's something I need to discuss with you both," Tristan said, his voice cutting through the domestic hum. The conversation ceased, giving way to a palpable tension that seemed to curl around us like smoke.

Reaching into his pocket, he pulled out two small objects that looked like hairpins, placing them on the table. "GPS trackers," he said matter-of-factly, his gaze meeting mine. "You'll keep them on you. It's a safety precaution."

Scarlett picked one up, her brow furrowing as she examined the device. "Is this necessary?"

"Given our history, Little Red, yes," Ethan interjected. "With the baby coming and all the unknowns, we can't be too careful."

Remaining silent, I held my own tracker, its cold metal casing sending a chill through my palm. Tristan leaned in closer, his breath ghosting over my skin as he pointed toward the barely visible button on the side. "That's what you press to send a signal of where you are. It'll notify Ethan and me. I wanted to make sure it was small and lightweight, so you could keep it on you. If anything happens... If you need help, we'll know where you are."

I nodded, slipping the device onto the band of my watch. "Thank you, Tristan," I managed to say, my voice a mere whisper. Appreciation for his vigilance warred with the gnawing fear that such precautions were not unfounded.

"Anything to keep you safe." Reaching out, he touched my hand, but it was the tenderness in his words that stirred something deep within me. "That's what's most important."

Once dinner was finished and the kitchen cleaned, the sun was already making its descent toward the horizon, darkening the spaces between the trees. I made my way through the house, picking up the toys that Evie had strewn all over the place while Tristan finished with Ethan downstairs. When I headed back to the kitchen to say my goodbyes, Scarlett's hands brushed mine as she reached for Eve's bag. "Caroline, why don't you let Evie stay over

tonight? She can have a slumber party with us and you...
Well, you can have some adult time."

Although Ethan and Scarlett lived nearby, it was rare that
Evie stayed at their house for the night. Not that she didn't
want to, or that they didn't want her to, but more because
after everything she'd been through, I never wanted to
leave her out of my sight. But I had to admit, the thought
of an evening untethered from motherly duties—a night
alone with Tristan—was as tempting as it was terrifying.
Plus, if that SUV came back, maybe it would be safer for
her to not be home.

I hesitated, a tangle of reluctance and yearning knotting in
my chest. "Are you sure?"

"Absolutely," she said, her deep brown eyes crinkling. "You
deserve it. Plus, it's not a school night. Go have yourself a
little fun for once."

I nodded, the weight of gratitude anchoring my smile and
overriding my hesitation as I peered into the living room
where Evie lay sprawled among her toys, completely consumed by the cartoon on the television. "Okay," I murmured, finally allowing the possibility of time alone with
Tristan to seep into my consciousness like rain through
parched soil. "I...um...but you'll call me if she wants to
come home? If she needs anything?"

"Of course, I will." Scarlett beamed at me, unaware of
the internal storm she'd unleashed. "You worry too much,
Caroline. Tonight, focus on yourself. Even if it's to watch a
movie and drink a glass of wine. Evie will be fine."

CHAPTER 14

The Phoenix

"Take a left here," I said, trying to force confidence into my voice as I pointed at a narrow road that veered off the main path. We'd only been in the car for about ten minutes, heading back to my cottage from Ethan and Scarlett's cabin, but the sun was setting, and I knew of a beautiful place to watch it. Still, my heart was pounding a million miles per hour against my ribcage. I didn't know what I was doing, but apparently, I was still going to do it, because my body knew I needed it even if my head was all over the place.

Tristan hesitated for a second, his hazel green eyes searching mine. "Are you sure?"

I nodded, butterflies fluttering in my stomach at the thought that maybe he realized what this was as much as I did. To be honest, I wasn't even sure if I knew what *this* was, but I couldn't deny the tension between us as he drove down the winding road. I found myself stealing glances at him, admiring the way his hands held the steering wheel with a confidence I didn't feel. There was chemistry between us, and I wasn't sure I wanted to fight it. The wedding band on my finger wasn't going to bring my husband back, no matter how much I wished otherwise.

"There's a lookout point down here to watch the sunset. I've never been there, but I've heard about it."

With a small smile, Tristan maneuvered the car down the winding road, following my lead. As the road narrowed and twisted, the trees on either side began to encroach in on us, creating almost a natural tunnel that blocked out all but the most determined slivers of the sun. When we reached the end of the road where there was a small empty parking lot, the world opened before us.

"Wow," Tristan said as he shifted the car into park. "This is incredible."

For a moment, we just sat there, but then he turned to look at me, the golden sunset reflecting off his glasses. "Do you want to get out?"

Tugging my lip between my teeth, I nodded, but before I could grab the handle, he was already on his way around the front of the car, opening my door. I took his hand and walked beside him to stand at the railing.

The forested valley below was untamed, a sea of mountains and lush green, crowned with wisps of clouds that seemed to dance in the evening light. A river snaked its way through the valley, its waters shimmering like liquid silver as it meandered through the dense forest below. As the wind whispered through the trees, carrying with it the scent of pine and wildflowers, an overwhelming sense of peace settled over me. In this place, miles from the world and its problems, it was just Tristan and me, sharing a moment that would forever be etched in my memory. I had been alone for so long, sheltering the fragile flame of my family from the harsh winds of the world. But in this moment, bathed in the afterglow of the setting sun, I realized that perhaps it was time to let someone else help tend the fire. Maybe, just maybe, it was time to let Tristan in—to let him stand beside me, not just as a guardian against the encroaching darkness, but as a companion to share in the light. At least, for one brave moment, it was a possibility my heart was offering to me, if that was what he wanted at all.

"Thank you for bringing me here." My voice was barely audible over the rustling leaves, but I knew he heard me, because when I turned my eyes up to look at him, he was watching me with an intensity that made my breath seize in my chest.

Reaching forward, he brushed a stray lock of hair from my face, tucking it behind my ear. The tenderness of his touch sent shivers down my spine, making my heart race uncontrollably. Unable to help myself, I leaned into his touch, my eyes falling shut for the briefest moment. With every touch, the walls I had meticulously built around myself seemed to crumble, brick by brick, right under his fingertips. I reopened my eyes after a heartbeat, not knowing what to say. "I'm sorry, it's just been so—"

And then his lips were on mine, gentle at first, as if testing the boundaries of this unfamiliar terrain, but they stole the words from my tongue. The taste of him was intoxicating, a heady blend of mint and possibility, igniting a fire within me that burned away the shadows of hesitation.

Three years. It had been three years since I'd had a man's lips on mine, and somewhere in my chest I knew there was a wound that still bled for Daniel, but when Tristan's hands found the small of my back, pulling me into the heat of his body, a surge of desire washed over me, potent and undeniable. Yet beneath the waves of passion from every slide of his tongue and press of his lips, there was a tremor of vulnerability, a soft undercurrent of fear at the thought of how much I stood to lose once more. Still, I yielded to him, my fingers threading through his already disheveled hair, clinging to him as though he was already mine.

When we finally broke apart, breathless and dazed, the echoes of my past grief hovered at the edges of my consciousness. Daniel's memory no longer cut as deep, but could it allow something new to grow amidst the ruins of my heart? It was an answer I didn't have, but I needed this. I needed something to help me feel again—to feel alive, to feel like a woman, desired and loved. There was so much I wanted, and I didn't know if Tristan was the man who could give it to me, or if he was even the man I wanted to, but I trusted him at that moment to make me feel again, and for that moment, it had to be enough.

Wrapping my arms around Tristan's back, I looked into his eyes, the vulnerability in them mirroring what hollowed my insides. "I'm scared," I admitted, the words tasting sour with truth. "Scared of losing again, of opening up and finding nothing but emptiness where love should be because I've already had my chance. I just don't want this to change us. Even if things don't work out, I need to know that we'll still be there for each other as friends."

Cupping my face, his thumbs wiped away the tears that had escaped unnoticed. "I know." The words were so soft that I felt them against my lips more than I heard them. "I can't promise you a future without pain or loss, Caroline. But I can promise you this—every moment with you is worth it, every second a chance to build something lasting. And no matter what, Caroline, I care about you. Nothing will ever change that. I'm not going to abandon you or your family."

Taking in his words and allowing them to process, I nodded, rising on the tips of my toes to kiss him again. This time it was without restraint, fueled by a hunger that had long lain dormant within me, and I moaned, needing—*wanting* more.

Sensing my need, or feeling his own, Tristan's hands roamed down my back, tracing the curve of my spine with a reverence that sent electricity cascading through my body. The rest of the world around us faded into insignificance as he pulled me into his arms, lifting me as though I was weightless and setting me down on the cool metal hood of his car. I arched into him, my fingers tugging gently on his hair, urging him to erase the empty spaces between us.

When we finally broke apart, a panicked look hit his eyes and he took a step back, the space between his eyebrows furrowing. The sudden rejection sent my heart crumbling to the ground. "Caroline, I'm so sorry. Maybe we're moving too—"

Before he could finish his statement, I reached for him, pulling his lips back to mine. I kissed him hard and deep, not letting up until he groaned against my lips. Only then did I pull back, staring into his eyes. "I'm not going to let you take any blame for this, Tristan. I asked you to bring me here because I wanted this. I want whatever you're willing to give to me... if only this once."

My bold words seemed to surprise him as much as they did me. His eyes flared, his hand immediately returning to my face. "Are you sure? I can just take you home. It's—"

I was already shaking my head. "The one thing I am sure about right now, Tristan, is that I want you to kiss me."

With no more arguments on his lips, his hand slid around to cup the back of my head and he tugged me forward, his lips unforgiving as they devoured mine. Frantic need pulsed between us as his hands found the hem of my shirt, yanking it over my head and discarding it on the hood of the car beside us. His touch was electric, sending jolts of awareness skittering across every inch of my body. As the soft fabric fell away, I couldn't help but think of the countless times I had undressed for Daniel, the intimacy of those moments forever etched into my memory, but my need was too strong to allow the guilt in. Not yet.

"Is this okay?" Tristan asked, his eyes locked on him as his fingers traced down the inside of my arm, leaving goose-flesh in its wake.

I nodded, a smile pulling up the corners of my mouth. "More than okay." The truth was, I had never felt more alive, at least not for as long as I could remember. Despite the weight of grief and loss that still clung to me like a shroud, there was something about his presence that made me feel as though I was emerging from a long, dark night into the light of a new day.

Reaching around, I unclasped my bra, dropping it on top of my shirt beside me. The chilly night air pebbled my nipples, turning Tristan's eyes dark as he took in the sight of me under the moonlit sky. His gaze was a caress, his touch gentle as he lifted his hands to my breasts, cupping them in his hands and rubbing his fingers along my nipples. Nothing about how he touched me was rushed, as though that moment between us was all that mattered.

Holding his eyes with mine, I reached for the hem of his shirt, fighting to steady my hands as I lifted it over his head. Everything about his sculpted body was perfect, as though he was carved from stone. My fingers itched to touch him, so I didn't deny myself. After so long without touching a man, I wanted my fingers on every inch of his perfect body. I ran my hand down his abs, loving how he hissed when I cupped the intimidating bulge through his jeans, but before I could unzip his pants and see what exactly he was hiding in there—genuinely afraid it may be too much for me—he peeled my hand away, laying me back on the hood and crawling over me.

My breath hitched as his mouth found the swell of my breast, his tongue tracing a path of fire over the sensitive flesh. With a moan, my fingers tightened in his hair as he lavished attention on one nipple and then the other. "I've been wanting to get my lips on these since I first saw you."

His breath was warm against my skin, but the words made me shiver. "You are so fucking beautiful."

The pounding of my heart was overwhelming, the need pulsing between my thighs ready to consume me. I wanted more. "Tristan..." It was barely a full word, but it was all I could manage as he sucked harder, grinding himself against my center. "Please."

Looking up at me, his eyes remained on mine as he kissed and sucked, his hand sliding down my stomach until it rested on the waistband of my pants. Even though my hips rolled against him, desperately searching for friction, his hand hesitated there, waiting for me to tell him to stop, but I didn't. I wouldn't.

"Are you sure?"

I knew he needed consent to continue, and I appreciated the out, but I didn't want to stop. Pulling myself up to sit, I reached for the button of his jeans, fumbling to undo them as I kissed him again. This time, he didn't push my hands away, but helped me instead, kicking off his boots and dropping his jeans to the ground.

"Fuck." The moment his thick length was free of its confines, my mouth went dry. He was still wearing his boxer briefs, but they had no hope of containing what this six-foot-four-inch man had below the belt. To be honest, I wasn't sure it would even fit inside of me, but I had every intention of trying.

I must have been staring, because unknown seconds or minutes later, his fingers slid beneath my chin, lifting my face to look at him. "Are you okay, Superwoman?"

Huffing a laugh, I nodded. "A little intimidated, but I'm okay. Yeah, I'm okay."

The questioning expression on his face morphed into something much smugger as he reached for my hand and wrapped it around his girth. "If a Superwoman like yourself can't handle me, then what hope do I have for anyone—"

"No." I cut that thought off before he could finish it, yanking him closer to me by his cock. "No one else will be handling you. I'll be just fine."

With a mischievous grin spreading across his lips, he leaned into me, his mouth taking mine in a dizzying kiss as he pulled me to my feet. I expected him to lay me back down on the car, or lift me up, but instead, he sank to his knees before me, his hands going to the laces of my boots. His eyes held my captive as he tugged off one and then the other, before his fingers hooked into the waistband of my tights. I didn't object as he slid them down, his hands gently caressing my thighs, his lips tracing their path. The vulnerability I felt as I stood there bare before him was both unsettling and exhilarating, like nothing I'd ever experienced before. His touch was electric, and his reverence for me—for us—shimmered in the air like an invisible thread binding us together in that moment.

As if mapping out the contours of my body, his fingers trailed up the length of my thigh, slowly, deliberately. I could feel the tension building within him, a simmering desire that mirrored my own. His eyes met mine, filled with a hunger that sent a shockwave of pleasure coursing through me. It was clear he wanted me as much as I wanted him.

The cool breeze played with the tendrils of my hair as Tristan's lips brushed my inner thigh, a feather-light caress that made my breath catch in my throat. His lips left a trail of heat in their wake, and with each kiss, each caress, he stripped away the layers of doubt and fear that had cloaked me for so long, revealing the raw, unfiltered desire that pulsed beneath my skin.

His tongue traced the delicate skin of my thigh, teasing me mercilessly as he teased apart my folds with his fingers. Moaning softly, my hips buckled involuntarily as he delved deeper, pressing a finger inside of me. His touch was pure magic, a heady cocktail of tenderness and sensuality that intoxicated me with every passing moment.

"Open for me, Superwoman. Let me taste you." I did as he asked, spreading my legs wider, my eyes following the top of his head as he leaned forward and slid his tongue through my wetness.

The first touch of his mouth to my overly sensitive flesh sent sparks into my vision and my legs dipped, nearly sending me onto the ground with him, but he reached around my thigh, holding me upright. As he licked and sucked on my clit, his fingers delved back inside of me, finding that place that promised blissful oblivion. My eyes fell shut and the breath burst from my mouth, my body arching toward him. The combination of the way his fingers moved inside me and how his tongue worked my clit was pure perfection, each touch leaving me breathless and trembling on the precipice of orgasm. It had been so long since I had even pleasured myself, so it didn't take long until I was clinging to him, my fingers digging into his shoulders as I rode his face and hand.

"Tristan. *Please.*" At my gasping cry, he doubled down, coaxing forth a storm of pleasure that threatened to consume me whole. My body trembled, the world around me fading away as I surrendered to the wave of pleasure that crashed over me, leaving me gasping and breathless in its wake as I collapsed onto his lap.

CHAPTER 15

The Phantom

As Caroline's body quivered with release, she dropped onto my lap and then slid to her knees on the ground beside me, kissing me as her hands eagerly slid my boxer briefs down my hips, freeing my throbbing cock. Her touch sent electric jolts coursing through my veins, threatening to set me on fire. The taste of her was still on my tongue as I slid it against hers, her hand gripping my cock causing me to hiss. My hips thrusted, forcing the friction my body demanded.

"I want to make you feel as amazing as you made me feel," she whispered, her voice thick with lust. I wanted to tell her that she already made me feel amazing, and that we could have gone home at that moment, and I would have been happy to give her more time. The last thing I wanted was for her to feel pressured into going all the way with me, but as she leaned forward and her lips wrapped around my cock, all those words came out as a groan of pleasure. The combination of her warmth and the cool breeze made my skin tingle, the juxtaposition of tenderness and urgency in her movements left me reeling, driving me closer and closer to the edge. It had been a while since I'd had lips around my cock, but I didn't want to blow my load too soon. I wanted to put her to sleep satisfied. I needed that just as much as she did.

"Caroline," I gasped, struggling to find the words to express the intensity of what I was feeling. "You...this...it's incredible...but I need to be inside you. *Now.*"

Not hesitating, she moved to climb over me, all five-foot-nothing of her, but I lifted her up, carrying her to the hood of my car and laying her down. She was stunning in the moonlight as I crawled over her, her eyes filled with a mix of vulnerability and desire, and I couldn't miss the trust she was placing in me. Pressing my lips against hers, the connection between us pulled us tighter, the fire igniting within me and burning away any lingering doubts or fears.

I reached for my jeans to grab a condom out of my wallet, but she placed her hand on mine, shaking her head. "I have an IUD. *Please.* I want to feel you...your skin."

Hesitating for only a moment, I nodded and leaned forward to kiss her. Gripping my cock, I guided it inside her, but only an inch before I realized I would have to go slow with her, at least at first. My little Superwoman was tiny, and she was tight, so although I wanted nothing more than to thrust inside and take her deep, I didn't want to hurt her. Holding my position, I allowed her to adjust to my size, moving slowly at first, savoring the feeling of her warmth enveloping me, swallowing her gasps with my kiss. With each thrust, I became increasingly lost in the moment, the rhythm of our bodies almost hypnotic.

As I began to pick up the pace, Caroline's moans grew louder, her body arching up to meet mine with each surge of my hips. Every slide of my cock against her slick flesh, the way her muscles clenched and squeezed me tighter, nearly brought tears to my eyes, the sensation almost too much to bear. Pulling away from her kiss, I cradled her face in my hands, looking deep into her blue eyes, wanting to see her lose control.

"Come for me, Superwoman."

"Harder. Tristan. *Please.*" The words were desperate, her fingers digging into my back as she begged for more. I was more than happy to give her what she wanted, especially after hearing my name on her lips while my cock was deep inside of her.

Lifting her hips, I worked her from a different angle, my thrusts becoming harder and faster until I knew I was bottoming out at her cervix. Her body trembled beneath me, her moans growing deeper and more guttural as her muscles clenched around me, pulling me even deeper into her. Pleasure more intense than anything I'd ever experienced had my entire body trembling as I pushed myself closer and closer to the edge.

Orgasm washing over her like a tsunami, Caroline cried out, the sound of her pleasure echoing through the mountains. The vise grip of her pussy around my cock was indescribable, her body convulsing beneath me as I continued to thrust, working toward my own edge. My movements became ragged, my legs nearly giving out from the sheer ecstasy as I came, releasing myself inside her. The feeling was overwhelming, my entire body tingling with pleasure as I collapsed onto her, my breath ragged and heavy.

Caroline wrapped her arms around me, her heart beating wildly against my chest. For a moment, we simply lay there on the hood of my car, our bodies entwined and our breaths mingling.

"That was...incredible," she whispered, nuzzling into my neck. "I never imagined it could be like this."

I kissed her gently on the forehead, and then again on her lips. "And I never imagined it could be you, but I'm so glad it is."

The moon was full as Caroline and I reluctantly pulled away from the lookout point up in the mountains, my body still tingling from what we'd done out there under the stars. Although we'd been flirting with each other for two days, I hadn't expected what would end up taking place between us. All I hoped was that she wouldn't end up regretting it.

Caroline rested her head on my shoulder as I drove, our fingers interlocking like pieces of a puzzle against my thigh. The night air was crisp and cool, but the silence in the car was charged, filled with words we'd yet to say. Although

I wanted more from her, I had no intention of pressuring her to give what she couldn't, and the not-knowing left the shadow of a pit in my chest, even in the afterglow of making love to her. If she was willing to give it, however, I wanted everything.

"Thank you for tonight," she whispered, her voice barely audible above the humming of the car engine.

I smiled down at her and kissed her on the top of her head, unsure of how to respond. The emotions that swirled within me felt too raw, too vulnerable to expose just yet. "Thank you for choosing to spend time with me."

As we drove through the winding roads that led back to Caroline's cottage, I was acutely aware of every bump and turn, each shift of gear causing a brief separation of our skin before we found our way back to one another.

The world outside seemed like a distant memory, the landscape and stars blurring together as my focus remained entirely on the woman beside me. I couldn't shake the feeling that something profound was happening, that this connection we shared went beyond physical attraction into something deeper, more meaningful.

"Almost there," I said, leaning down to kiss the top of her head again.

Caroline looked up at me, her eyes filled with a tenderness that made my heart ache. "I'm glad you're here, Tristan."

"Me too."

The cottage's warm glow cast a welcoming light as we pulled up, the gravel crunching beneath the tires as I parked the car. For a moment, we sat in silence, breathing the only sound in the car.

"Home, sweet home," she whispered, her eyes locked onto mine.

Climbing out of the car, I walked around to the other side and opened her door, resting my hand on the small of her back as I followed her toward the front door. The minute we stepped onto the porch, as though we were teens getting home from a date, I couldn't resist any longer. Leaning over, I captured her lips in a kiss that stirred my soul, setting my world on fire. With my arms wrapped around her, I pressed her against the outside of the house, caging her in as I devoured her mouth.

"Come. Shower," she gasped against my mouth, tugging me toward the door. After all the time we'd just spent on the ground and the hood of my car, I didn't object. My need for her was so intense that not even the prospect of chilly water could dampen it.

We stumbled through the door, nearly forgetting to close it behind us. Our lips never parted as we made our way down the dimly lit hallway, every step bringing us closer to the bedroom, our clothes discarded along the way.

As soon as the water began to cascade over us, all thoughts of restraint vanished. The sensation of her wet skin against mine only served to fan the flames of passion, our hands urgent as we touched each other.

"Fuck, Superwoman," I breathed into her ear, my fingers tangling in her long, damp hair. "You're fucking incredible." She was a petite little thing, but her curves were succulent. All I wanted was to lay her on her stomach and eat a meal right off her plump backside.

Wrapping my hand around her tiny waist, I pressed her against the wall of the shower, mesmerized at how the water trailed down her full breasts. Unable to help myself, I leaned forward and took her nipple into my mouth, not caring that the deluge from the shower would probably drown me.

Her response was a moan, her nails digging into my back as she pressed herself even closer to me. I lavished attention on her breasts, her neck, returning to her lips and kissing her with a frantic, hungry pace. Though I'd already been inside her, I wanted to be inside her again—to go as deep as I could and stay for a while. But even in our insatiable passion, there were moments when our touches softened beneath the spray of the water, when our lips met in tender, lingering caresses that spoke of a growing emotional bond just as powerful as our physical one. All I wanted was to hear more of those little sounds she made when I made her feel good, but I wanted her heart more.

Although we could have easily allowed our passion in the shower to burn hotter until I had her taking my cock against the tiles, it was about more than that for me, so I wanted to make sure she understood that. She wasn't just a warm hole for me to come inside. Caroline was special—someone who was worth forever. Plus, she was small and tight, and the last thing I wanted to do was hurt her. So, although my cock was painfully erect the entire time, I'd washed her hair and body for her, caressing her curves with reverence. I stepped out of the shower without taking her again. There would be time for that later.

Lighting the fireplace in the living room, we settled down on the plush rug in front of the fire, the soft glow of the flames casting flickering shadows across the walls. Wrapped in a thick blanket, Caroline snuggled against my side, her head resting on my chest as I held her close. We shared a bottle of Pinot Noir between us, passing it back and forth as we sipped straight from the bottle. The warmth of the fire and the brush of her skin against mine sparked a sense of contentment I hadn't felt in years.

Caroline's fingers traced idle patterns on my bare chest, the crackling of the fire providing a soothing backdrop to our shared silence as we watched the flames. The weight of unspoken words hung heavy in the air, yet in that moment, words felt unnecessary.

"I never expected this," she murmured softly, her eyes fixed on the dancing flames. "To feel so...at peace."

Her vulnerability warmed my heart, and I turned to look at her, the flickering firelight casting shadows on her face, accentuating the curves and angles that made her uniquely beautiful.

"Me neither," I admitted, my voice low. "But I wouldn't change a thing."

She smiled, a genuine expression that reached her eyes and filled me with a sense of belonging I had never experienced before, but I was scared to lose.

"Tell me about your family."

The crackling of the fire seemed to hush for a moment, as if the flames themselves were eager to hear the secrets I held within. I hesitated, not out of reluctance but out of a deep-rooted need to choose my words carefully. "I have no blood family left," I confessed, my gaze turning introspective as memories long buried resurfaced. "My parents died in a car crash when I was young. I spent a few years in the foster care system before I ran away. That's when Legacy found me and took me in. He taught me everything about hacking, about surviving. He was more of a father than anyone else I'd ever known."

Caroline's hand found mine, offering silent comfort amid my pain. There was no question how much she had of her own. "I'm so sorry, Tristan," she whispered, her fingers intertwined with mine as if to anchor me to the present. Her touch soothed wounds I had carried for so long, wounds that still throbbed with the ache of loss, but I knew she'd lost so much more.

"It's okay," I reassured her, my voice soft but steady. "I've made my peace with it over the years. But the absence of family, of roots...it leaves a void that nothing else can fill."

Caroline nodded, her head resting on my chest. "Ethan and I lost our parents the same way...the same way I lost Daniel. My brother and I were teens too—him sixteen and me eighteen." Taking a sip of her wine, she continued, "From that moment on, it was just...us. Overnight, I had to figure out how to keep him out of trouble, how to be strong for the both of us, but it wasn't easy." A laugh huffed from her mouth as she shook her head. "No matter what I did, he always seemed to find trouble. I was still a kid myself, trying to navigate a world that seemed so much darker without them."

In a world filled with families —people who had others to depend on—I understood what it was like to live without that. I understood her.

Pulling her closer, I kissed her on the cheek, my heart aching for the pain she'd endured, and for how many inadequacies she seemed to see in herself when all I saw was strength and resilience. "You stood up for your brother and took the place of a parent when you still needed them yourself. Be proud of yourself for all you did, because I know your brother is, and I'm sure your parents would be too."

Although I felt her nod against my chest, I knew there was still a part of her that would never give herself the slack she deserved, and that broke my heart. "Life hasn't been easy for either of us, but somehow, we found each other in all this darkness. Maybe that's what makes this connection between us so special...because we understand each other's pain."

CHAPTER 16

The Phoenix

The warmth of the fire seeped into my skin as I nestled against Tristan's chest, the slow beat of his heart soothing my troubled mind. An open bottle of red wine sat between us, half-empty, along with an assortment of snacks we'd been picking through.

"I still worry about Evie's health," I admitted as I watched the flickering flames, hating hearing the words aloud. "Every day, I wake up afraid her cancer might have returned."

Tristan pressed a tender kiss to my hair, his arms tightening around me. "She's been in remission for a while now. Her prognosis looks good, right?"

Taking another sip of wine, I sighed but nodded. The memory of Evie's pallid face and frail body during her time in the hospital still haunted my dreams. "Yes. But I'm her mommy, I'll always worry. What if I can't protect her from this? What if I fail her?"

"That's only natural." His fingers traced slow circles over my back, making me want to curl around him like a cat. "You've been through so much. It's understandable you'd feel anxious."

His empathy only made my eyes burn with tears I refused to shed. Even knowing my history, he still wanted me, but that didn't change how much of a burden I felt. He was young, and deserved someone with less baggage, but even thinking that sent a throbbing pain straight through my chest. Staring into the fire, a million thoughts and emotions swirled through my mind, and none of them wanted to let whatever this was between us go.

"Thank you," I whispered, leaning closer against his side. "For being here. For caring about me, scars, and all."

He pressed his lips against my temple, his breath warm against my skin. "Every part of you is beautiful and precious to me. Scars and all."

His words melted the remaining chill in my heart, filling it with warmth. Turning toward him, I wrapped my arms around his neck, bringing his lips to mine. An intense mix of longing and bittersweet desire pulsed through me as our mouths connected. His lips were soft like velvet, tender and demanding at the same time, and I matched his passion eagerly. The kiss tasted of wine and the smoky warmth of the fireplace, a heady blend that intoxicated me more than the wine flowing through my system.

The kiss intensified, our bodies instinctively drawing closer, seeking the warmth of skin on skin. His hands roamed over my curves as though he was memorizing the landscape of my form, leaving shivers in the wake of his touch. My fingers tangled in his hair, tugging slightly, making him hiss.

Wrapping his arm around me, Tristan laid me back onto the rug. I went willingly, craving his touch. His body pressed into mine, hard muscle, and soft warmth. My hands slipped around him, splaying across his toned back.

So much loss. So much pain. In Tristan's embrace, those sharp edges dulled. The empty spaces inside filled. Three years of grief seemed to fade into the shadows as passion lit a new flame.

"You're so soft," Tristan whispered, his lips trailing down my neck. Pleasure sparked under his touch, chasing away the darkness.

A low moan escaped me as he found the edge of my nightshirt, slipping beneath the fabric. Trailing his hands up my ribcage, his fingers brushed the underside of my breast. I arched into his touch, wanting him higher.

"I want this," he said, voice rough with desire. "I want you."

Palming the back of his head, I brought his mouth to mine, whispering against his lips, "Then take me."

With my invitation the last of his restraint shattered, and he pulled my shirt over my head, discarding the fabric to the side. I lay bare from the waist up before him on the rug, heart pounding as his gaze roamed over my body, but there was no judgment in his eyes, only heat, and something else I couldn't decipher—or maybe I wasn't ready to.

"You're beautiful." Reaching forward, his fingers traced along my collarbone. Down between my breasts. Along the curve of my waist. Every touch left fire in its wake, desire building inside me like the flames in the hearth.

When his lips followed the path his hands had taken, I thought I might come undone right then and there. Soft kisses and teasing bites along sensitive skin ignited my nerves. I tangled my hands in his hair, holding him to me, craving more but dreading the loss of his mouth on my flesh.

Lingering at my breasts, his tongue teased my nipples, sucking and nibbling as my body rolled beneath him, needing friction between my thighs as badly as I needed air.

"Please," I gasped, not even sure what I was asking for. More, less, everything, nothing. I only knew I needed him, all of him, and I needed it now.

Eyes locking on mine, his hands slid down to the waist of my panties, fingers hooking in the elastic. He hesitated there, a question in his gaze. There was no question.

I nodded, unable to find my voice, but I knew what I wanted. There were no more barriers left between us, no more secrets kept or desires unfulfilled. At least for tonight, I was his and he was mine, and together we would find solace in the flames.

With his eyes still on mine, darkened by desire, he slid my panties down my legs, settling between them. I reached for him, but he caught my hands, pinning them above my head.

"Not yet. Let me taste you first, Superwoman. I need you back on my tongue."

Then he was on me, tongue teasing and tasting, pushing me higher and higher. After the time we spent on the mountain lookout, he knew enough about my body to know every place that brought me pleasure, and he lavished them all with attention. I twisted beneath him, tension coiling tighter and tighter, release hovering just out of reach.

When he increased his suction, focusing all his attention on my clit, I shattered, crying out as ecstasy flooded my veins. He gentled his touch once I'd fallen over the edge, easing me through the aftershocks until I lay limp on the rug, heart pounding.

Before I had even come back down to earth, Tristan lifted me into his arms, carrying me down the hall to my bedroom. I nestled against his chest, sated yet craving more.

When we got into my bedroom, the moon was the only light as it filtered in through the window. He laid me on the bed, following me down to cover my body with his. I wrapped my legs around his waist, urging him closer, gasping as he slid inside me an inch, but Tristan was impossibly large, so taking him all the way was a slow process.

"You're so fucking big, hacker."

Hooking his arm around my back, he chuckled as he rolled onto his back, leaving me to straddle his hips—giving me control. I braced my hands on his chest, leaning down to kiss him as I rolled my hips to take him deeper. With every inch that stretched me more than should have been normal, I hissed, legs trembling. "You can take it, baby. You took it all the way already tonight."

The corner of his lips lifted in a smug grin as his hands gripped my waist and he braced my weight, helping guide me up and down on his length. My head fell back as his massive cock invaded every empty space inside me, claiming it as his own. When I looked back down, our gazes locked, breaths mingling, and the affection I saw in his eyes was painfully raw. In that moment, with pleasure making even my face tingle, I gave myself over to him, and when release came, it was shattering in its sweetness.

CHAPTER 17

The Phoenix

Tristan's breath was warm against my neck when I woke up the following morning with his arm draped over my waist, our legs tangled together under the sheets. It should have been comforting, but it only amplified the thrumming guilt gnawing at the edge of my conscience as I realized we had crossed a line we could never uncross. In the light of morning the fog cleared, and Daniel's face flashed in my mind, sending a sharp pang of betrayal straight through me.

"Morning," Tristan murmured, his voice raspy and thick with sleep as he tightened his grip around me.

"Good morning," I whispered back, forcing the words out through the tight knot in my throat.

"Did you sleep well?" His hazel eyes met mine, searching for more than what he was asking.

"Um, yes," I lied, not wanting to admit that I had woken up at some point in the middle of the night, questioning everything I knew about love and loyalty. After three years, the ghost of my late husband still lingered, a silent witness to my indiscretions, and I didn't know how to make it leave so I could move on.

"Good." Smiling softly, he pressed a gentle kiss on my forehead. "I'm gonna take a shower, if that's okay."

I nodded, forcing a smile to cross my lips even though I didn't know if it was real. "Of course. Make yourself at home."

I couldn't help but watch him as he walked to the bathroom, the lean muscles of his back moving gracefully beneath his skin as he disappeared behind the door. There was a lot I didn't know, but I couldn't deny how attractive he was, and how much I craved his touch.

With Tristan gone, I pulled the sheets tighter around me, trying to make sense of my conflicting emotions. Was it so wrong to feel so drawn to him when my heart still ached for Daniel? My thoughts swirled like an unforgiving tempest, offering no solace or resolution.

But as much as I tried to resist it, there was no denying that Tristan had awakened something within me—something that had lain dormant since Daniel's passing. It scared me, but at the same time, I couldn't ignore the comfort and connection I felt with him.

As the sound of water cascading in the shower reached my ears, I closed my eyes and allowed myself to breathe, but I didn't remain there long, not with the text from Scarlett saying that Evie was asking to go home and play with the kitty.

So, although I would've liked to stay curled up in bed longer, I slid out of bed, pulled on some tights and a shirt, and headed out into the main living area. I needed time to process what had happened between us. How much time? I wasn't sure. I just needed...*time*.

When I entered the kitchen, I spotted Houdini beneath the table, but he popped up as I walked in, curling around my ankles. "Good morning, you little magician." Reaching down, I scratched behind his ear. His appreciative purrs brought a smile to my face even when my heart was hurting. "Let's get you fed."

With the black cat following my every move as if he was silently urging me to hurry up, or judging me like I was judging myself, I opened a can of his food and set the plate on the ground.

Once Houdini was eating his meal and the coffee dripped, I leaned against the counter, my heart falling back into the tangle of emotions stirring inside me. I stood there for a moment as I listened to the sound of the shower down the hall, my mind spinning as I tried to process the conversation Tristan and I needed to have. Yet, the thought of discussing it with him filled me with apprehension, as if uttering the words would make the situation all too real. The worst part was that the sex had been great—impossibly so. There was incredible chemistry between us, and his willingness to put himself in the line of fire for my family was something most people would die for. There were so many reasons for me to explore something deeper with Tristan, but my damn heart... I just didn't know if I was ready.

The coffee maker gurgled as I cracked eggs into a pan, my thoughts churning endlessly. I had sacrificed everything to keep Evie safe, including my own happiness. How could one night with Tristan unravel all my resolve?

"I'm sorry, Daniel," I whispered, just in case he could still hear me. "I never meant for this to happen." The words echoed hollowly in the empty kitchen, a vain attempt to assuage my guilt. But it was too late for apologies. I had opened the floodgates, and there was no going back. The only question was whether I would drown in the deluge or find a way to stay afloat in the churning sea of emotions Tristan had awakened in me.

The floorboards creaked behind me and I tensed, my heart leaping into my throat. I didn't dare turn around, afraid of what I might see in Tristan's eyes. His bare feet padded across the kitchen tiles, coming to a stop a few feet away from me. Avoiding looking at him, I kept my gaze fixed on the eggs, pushing them around the pan.

The silence stretched between us, fragile and tenuous, as if the wrong word might shatter it into a million pieces. I swallowed hard, acutely aware of his presence behind me. His scent enveloped me, sandalwood mixed with the scent of body wash, evoking memories of our night together that I now longed to forget, because I didn't know how else to forgive myself.

"Caroline?" Tristan's voice caused me to flinch, and I had no choice but to turn around and look at him. Dressed in a clean pair of dark jeans, beads of water still clung to his toned chest. One thing I couldn't deny was how handsome he was, even when he wasn't trying. "Do you need any help?"

"Uh, no, I'm fine," I replied, trying to sound casual despite the way my pulse raced at the sight of him. "Breakfast is almost ready."

"Alright." Lips tipping up in a smile, he pulled a black T-shirt on and crossed the room, taking a seat at the table. "It smells good."

"Thank you." My fingers fumbled with the toaster, nearly dropping a slice of bread onto the floor.

When everything was done, I plated the eggs and toast and brought it to the table, forcing my lips to lift in a half smile. "Here you go."

His eyes locked on me as he took a sip of his coffee and smiled at me again, my blasphemous mind remembering how those lips felt all over my body. There was nowhere they hadn't kissed. "Thanks."

For the next several minutes, we ate in silence, the air thick with unspoken words, and I couldn't help but steal glances at him as he ate, wishing things could be less complicated.

"Tristan, about last night..." I began, the words lodging in my throat.

Setting his fork down, he placed his hand on mine across the table, looking directly into my eyes. The way he seemed to look straight through my skin left me so much more vulnerable than I ever allowed myself to be. "We don't have to talk about it right now if you're not ready."

I closed my eyes briefly. My heart ached with uncertainty, longing for resolution but fearing what it might mean. "Are you sure?"

"Of course," he assured me, his gaze softening. "I told you before—I don't want you to feel forced into any- thing you're not comfortable with. I'll be here when you're ready."

A heavy sigh escaped my lips, the weight of our unresolved conversation settling on my shoulders like an oppressive fog, but before I could respond, the sound of a car engine and laughter outside froze my thoughts in place. Evie.

Before I was ready, the front door burst open and Evie raced into the kitchen, a toothy smile glued across her face. "Mommy, look what Uncle Ethan gave me!" In her hand was a pink unicorn, its mane striped with a rain- bow of bright colors. Ethan and Scarlett followed close behind, a box of pastries in Ethan's hand from my favorite bakery. The fragile moment between Tristan and I had been shattered into a million pieces and scattered to the four winds. My stomach dropped as I realized we were no longer alone—no longer able to settle things, even if we wanted to. At least not for the moment. I swallowed the lump in my throat and forced a smile, pushing aside my turbulent emotions to focus on Evie.

I held out my arms, wrapping them around her as she rushed forward. "I love it, nugget. It's very pretty."

Murmuring a quick hello, Tristan walked to the sink and began washing the dishes. I bit my lip, a pang of guilt hitting me at his thoughtfulness. He always seemed to know what needed to be done, anticipating problems before they arose. If only I could be so pragmatic about our relationship—or whatever this was.

Seeming unphased by the tension in the room—or at least pretending to be—Ethan and Scarlett settled in at the table, Scarlett helping Evie assemble a puzzle on the worn wooden surface. I busied myself making fresh coffee, the domesticity of the moment at odds with the riot of emotions inside me.

We fell into an easy rhythm, the conversation flowing around me while I remained apart, trapped in the turmoil of my thoughts. Tristan's eyes met mine across the room, a question in their depths that I didn't dare answer. Instead, I looked away, a flush heating my cheeks.

The day passed in a blur of forced cheer and pretend normalcy. Baking cookies with Scarlett, playing board games with Evie, all while stealing glances at Tristan and wondering if I was the only one affected by the change in our dynamic. His affection seemed unchanged, a steady warmth that did nothing to alleviate my guilt.

Once night fell and Evie was tucked into bed, an awkward silence descended. Tristan and Ethan had been working on my cottage's security system all day, but after dinner, we'd all sat down in the living room in front of the television. Ethan put a fight on, and although he and Tristan seemed completely engaged in the violence on the screen, I could not get the thoughts of the night before out of my mind.

Feeling like I may just climb out of my skin, I stood abruptly, nearly knocking over my glass of wine. "I should get to bed. Evie will be up early."

From across the room, Tristan's gaze was piercing, seeing far too much. I refused to meet his eyes, instead bidding a hasty goodnight to Ethan and Scarlett. If Tristan came to me after they left, I didn't know if I would have the strength to turn him away. The thought filled me with equal parts anticipation and dread. I was in too deep and there seemed no straightforward way out. The path before me was shrouded in shadows, the future uncertain. All I knew was that everything had changed.

For the next few hours, I tossed and turned, sleep eluding me. As I waited for the darkness to take me, the clock ticked past midnight, then an hour later.

Finally giving up, I crept down the hall in search of a glass of water. The house was dark and silent, moonlight filtering through the windows to cast shadows across the floor.

As I entered the kitchen, I froze. Tristan stood by the sink, his shirtless back to me. He turned to the sound of my footsteps, eyes gleaming behind his glasses.

Unsure what to say, I licked my lips, my heart stuttering at the sight of him. The air between us was so charged, it pricked my skin.

Setting down his glass, he took a step toward me. "Caroline."

I shook my head, pulse racing. "Don't. *Please*." If he touched me, if he said my name like that again, I knew my resolve would crumble. In my frame of mind, I couldn't give in to my desire to be close to him, no matter how badly I might have wanted to.

"You regret what happened." His voice was flat, guarded. It was impossible for me to miss the hurt in his eyes before he turned away. "I understand. It won't happen again."

"Tristan, I—" The words caught in my throat. How could I possibly explain the tangled mess of emotions inside me? It was too complicated—impossible to put into words.

When he looked at me again, his expression was clear, which only shattered my heart more, because I knew he was doing it for me. "You don't owe me anything, Caroline. I'm the one who crossed the line. I took advantage of you at a vulnerable moment, and I regret that more than I can say." Setting his glass in the sink, he dipped his chin, a sad smile pulling up the side of his mouth. "Goodnight, Superwoman."

Pressing a hand over my heart as a fresh wound ripped open in my chest, I watched his retreating form disappear into the dark hallway. What had I done? In my desire to protect myself, I'd hurt a great man—a friend—someone I knew had honorable intentions. All he'd wanted to do was be there for me, to take care of me, and I'd hurt him.

I stood in the kitchen long after he'd disappeared into the guestroom, adrift, anchorless, and alone, just like I always was.

CHAPTER 18

The Phantom

As the last wire clicked into place, the small LED on the control panel blinked to life, casting an emerald glow across my fingers. I let out a breath, trying to release some of the tension in my chest that shouldn't have been there after the night I'd had just over twenty-four hours earlier, but Caroline had barely spoken to me since, making it very clear she thought what we'd done together was a mistake. I didn't agree, and although we didn't know each other well, we had an undeniable connection, so her cold shoulder cut deep.

"Should keep any threats at bay," I murmured, more to myself than anyone else. Ethan grunted his approval from the doorway, his light blue eyes scanning the monitor we'd set up for all the cameras. We'd been working on Caroline's security system for two days, beefing up the system she'd already had in place. This way, even when she was alone, I hoped she would sleep easier.

When Ethan and I finished with the cameras, I stepped into the kitchen where I found Caroline staring out the window, her reflection a ghost upon the glass. It took a moment before she seemed to notice my presence, her body stiffening even though she didn't turn to look at me.

"Hey. Security system looks good." I said, my voice low as I stepped farther into the room. "Are you okay?" Neither of us were okay. I knew that, but I didn't know what else to say.

In her reflection, I saw a small smile lift the side of her mouth, but it didn't reach her eyes. "Fine. Just tired." Her voice was devoid of its usual melody, clipped like the wings of a caged bird. Longing and regret pierced through me, tightening my chest.

Although I knew sleeplessness wasn't the thief stealing the softness from her tone, and all I wanted to do was make her smile, I nodded. "That's understandable."

Behind us, Ethan and Scarlett were setting up a board game at the table with Evie, and I couldn't help but feel like an outsider, a specter hovering on the fringes of their happiness. And Caroline, the woman who had somehow slipped past my defenses, whose taste was all I could think about, now seemed as unreachable as the stars above.

"Tristan," Scarlett called, snapping me back to the present. "Are you staying for dinner?"

Glancing at Caroline, who was still staring sightlessly out of the window, I shook my head. "Appreciate it, but I think I'll pass. I need to head back soon." My words felt hollow, even to my own ears. The idea of sitting at a table, surrounded by the warmth of family—next to a woman I wanted to touch more than anything—while grappling with my own sense of isolation, was more than I could bear.

"Suit yourself," Scarlett replied with a shrug, but there was no sign of offense in her dismissal, thankfully. The last thing I wanted them to think was that I didn't want to be around them. I just thought it would be best if I wasn't for a while.

Retreating to the guest bedroom, I gathered up mine and Houdini's things, hoping Caroline would walk into the room and ask me to stay, but she didn't. The mountain air, crisp and tinged with the scent of pine, filtered through the open window, a subtle whisper of the freedom I was about to claim, but it was suffocating. Still, I zipped the bag with a steady hand, the possible finality of the motion reverberating through my chest. I was leaving, but every fiber of my being was screaming for me to stay, because I realized that once I left, she may not want to see me again. Just the thought of it was like a jagged blade to the heart.

"Tristan? Are you leaving?" Caroline's voice broke through the silence, sending my stomach into a flip. *Hope.*

I turned, facing her and Evie, the child's bright eyes so much more joyful than her mother's guarded expression.

"Hey. Yes. I have some stuff I need to take care of back in Atlanta." The words tasted bitter on my tongue, and I think we both knew I didn't really need to leave, but I felt like I had to. "Just for a few days."

A flicker of something—confusion, perhaps even hurt—crossed Caroline's features before she masked it with the practiced stoicism of a woman who had endured far too much loss.

Walking over to Evie, I crouched down to get more on her eye level. "Be good for your mom, okay?"

She threw her arms around my neck, hugging me tightly. "Will you come back soon?"

I held her close for a moment longer, throat tightening. "Of course I'll come back. Houdini and me. You can get rid of me that easily, Captain."

Although it wasn't genuine, I forced a smile onto my face, glancing back up at Caroline as I stood. I ached to pull her into my arms but resisted. "Take care of yourself." Unable to hide my emotions as well as hoped, my voice was rough.

She dipped her head. "Okay, well, be careful driving back," she murmured, her voice just as unsure. Still, she didn't ask why I was leaving, or when I would return, but I could hear the undercurrent of something unsaid, a quarry of emotions she wasn't yet ready to voice.

Dipping my chin once more, I said goodbye to Scarlett and Ethan, grabbed my cat, and walked out into the twilight, the sky painted with streaks of fading light as day bled into night.

Once Houdini was inside the car, I lingered by the driver's side of my Mustang for a moment, stalling, hoping Caroline would stop me. She stood a few steps away, her arms wrapped around herself despite the evening's mild chill. "Tristan," she whispered, the name hanging between us.

"Caroline." My reply mirrored hers, a soft echo in the growing darkness. Our eyes locked, and for a heartbeat, there seemed to be a silent plea for understanding, a flicker of something that might have been had circumstances been different. But words failed us, and the moment stretched taut, making it difficult to breathe. When I'd lost all hope that she would speak again, she shifted on her feet, moving closer to the door, telling me the conversation wasn't going any further.

"Can you text me when you get home, let me know you made it home safely?" she finally said, her voice imbued with a strength that belied the tremble in her lips.

Dipping my chin, I offered her a half-smile, when all I wanted to do was kiss her. "Yeah. I can do that."

With one last look, I opened the car door, the creaking hinges sounding louder than I remembered in the silent air. The engine roared to life when I turned the key, the rumble not as satisfying as it always had been. This time, I wasn't ready to drive away, but I wasn't going to force her into anything she wasn't ready for. So, with a heavy heart, I glanced through the rearview mirror at her silhouette, where she still stood with her arms wrapped around her middle and eased my car onto the street. Within moments, the cottage and Caroline were nothing more than a speck in the mirror, then gone altogether, swallowed by the encroaching night.

Solitude surrounded me as I entered my apartment, the space seeming cavernous and empty. I sat on the edge of my bed, staring at the floor. The security system was in place, Evie was in remission, and Caroline was safe with her family. I should have been content with that because she didn't owe me anything, but I felt so unbelievably lost.

Grabbing my cell, I sent a quick text to Caroline as she'd requested, the words "made it home safe" the only thing I could muster. For several minutes, I watched the screen, but no response came.

A hollow ache settled inside my chest where the happiness from being intimate with Caroline had been. Part of me wanted to cut my losses and fall back into who I was before—who I'd always been—but I realized with clarity that I didn't want to lose her. I didn't want to lose any of them. In such a brief period of time, they had become my family, filling the void that had existed for so long.

And now I was alone again, but I'd had a taste of being close to someone amazing, and I didn't think I could go back to the way things were before.

Shaking my head, I stood up and walked to my computer lab, needing to busy my hands, needing to get back to work. I had already lingered there too long, my thoughts consumed by a woman who held my heart in her hands, whether she realized it or not. A woman whose family I was determined to protect, no matter the cost.

For the next few hours, I dove into the familiar world of code, needing to update my other clients, losing myself in the challenges that had once brought me solace. But there was no escape from the thoughts of Caroline that persisted at the edges of my mind—the memory of her smile, the sound of her laughter, the way she looked at me with those big blue eyes and saw into my soul.

Fingers faltering on the keyboard, I rubbed the back of my neck, frustration mounting. I couldn't focus, couldn't think of anything but her and how we'd left things. The time we had shared replayed itself like a movie in my head, my brain trying to understand where it had gone wrong. Although I knew she still grieved for her husband, I just couldn't shake the worry that it was something I'd done.

Abandoning my work, I took a quick shower and climbed into bed. Exhaustion settled into my bones, but sleep eluded me. My mind refused to quiet, racing with concern for Caroline's safety on top of the confusion about the drastic shift in her temperature.

Closing my eyes, I swallowed against the ache in my throat. Tomorrow, I thought. Tomorrow, I needed to find a way to close the chasm between us, because Caroline was worth fighting for.

CHAPTER 19

The Phantom

T he next morning, I woke to no messages from Caroline on my phone, but when I stumbled into my lab with a cup of coffee in hand, there was an alert flashing on one of my monitors. Bleary eyed and yawning, I dropped into my chair and clicked on the message waiting in my encrypted inbox from ShadowRunner.

As the words came into focus, dread pooled in my stomach, cold and heavy. Someone had placed bounties on Scarlett and her father, revealing details about their appearances, last known locations, and a significant reward for information leading to their captures.

Heart racing, I read the message again, panic and fear mingling. I took a deep breath, doing my best to calm down, knowing any rash decisions could put them in greater danger, but my veins were filled with live wires.

My fingers flew across the keyboard, scrolling endlessly through the darkness. Somewhere in the tangled web was a trail leading to Umberto Aresco. The ShadowRunner's message mentioned him by name, which meant he was involved in the threats against Scarlett and Ivy—if ShadowRunner was telling the truth.

I didn't know much about Aresco, but after hours of searching, one name kept appearing again and again in hidden chat logs and encrypted messages: *Cinder*.

The name echoed in my mind as I leaned back in my chair, eyes burning from staring at the screens for so long, but my searching had paid off. The trail of clues, as entangled as it was, led back to only one conclusion: Umberto Aresco was Cinder, but that wasn't the worst part. Aresco had been on the FBI's radar for years but had remained untouchable, a ghost in the machine who didn't leave loose ends. He engaged in organized crime across the East Coast at the highest levels, and he wanted Scarlett and Ivy captured or eliminated.

My stomach churned as the truth sank in. Being related to the Italian mafia, he had eyes and ears everywhere, informants who would do anything for the right price. I didn't know why the Italian mafia had a stake in New Orleans organized crime, but if he was truly after them, they wouldn't last long, not on their own. Even Ethan would be out of his league if Aresco was truly after his wife and father-in-law.

Heart pounding against my ribs, I pulled off my glasses and ran a hand through my hair. There was still a lot I didn't know, but I needed to call Ethan and tell him what I found out. I dialed his number on a secure line, and it only rang once before a familiar voice answered.

"Talk to me." Ethan's voice was clipped, impatient, clearly suspecting it was not a social call.

"It's worse than we thought," I said without preamble. "Umberto Aresco is involved. Italian mobster. He's been using the alias 'Cinder' and has put a bounty on Scarlett and Ivy. Alive or dead. I don't know how much time we have before his men find them."

Silence. Then a muffled curse. "How did you uncover this?"

I rubbed the back of my neck, feeling the tension coiled there. "A lot of digging. It took time to trace everything back to him, but the signs are irrefutable. I still need to dig more into his connections to the New Orleans gangs, but from what I've found thus far, it looks like gangs from the North have illegal shipments coming in through the port of Orleans. Delacroix's gang was like the troll under the bridge, more or less. Everyone else pays a toll for their products to pass."

"Shit. Alright." Ethan's voice turned steely, authoritative. "I know we've already wiped Scarlett's digital footprint, but search again, make sure we didn't miss anything." He went quiet for a moment, and I knew he was pacing.

"You got it, boss. Anything else?"

"Monitor the FBI's movements and communications. See what they know and if you can find out where Ivy is being kept. We need to get to him before Aresco's men do."

Adrenaline surged through my veins, and I tapped on my mouse, needing to do something with my pent-up energy. "Consider it done. I can send an anonymous tip that Ivy's location has been compromised—force the feds to move him again. Maybe that will buy more time."

"That's a good idea." His tone softened for a moment—my friend coming through. "Call me as soon as you have any updates. And Tristan, be careful. If these assholes find out who you are and that you're involved, they won't hesitate to take you out too."

Dread sent my heart into my stomach, but it was an inevitability I'd already considered. Nothing about this situation was safe. "With all due respect, boss, he'll have to catch me first."

Ethan huffed out a laugh. "Godspeed, Phantom.

A moment later, the line went dead. I sat there for a moment, running a search for Scarlett's name that would take some time to finish, and sending the tip I'd mentioned to the authorities. Fresh anxiety tightened my chest—worry for my friends and heartbreak over Caroline. I needed to move.

With a sigh, I secured the earbuds in my ears and walked down the hall, pushing the door open to my home gym. I never needed a guest room, so instead of a bed, it was filled with equipment—a treadmill, row machine, and weights, the basics so I didn't need to use a public gym.

As the music pulsed through my earbuds, I worked through my routine. The sound of my footsteps on the mat, the grip of the weights in my hands, and the burn of my muscles echoed in my mind as I went through the motions. I pushed harder, faster, my heart pounding in rhythm with the heavy metal music that screamed in my ears. Sweat dripped down my forehead as the adrenaline rushed through my veins. Yet, amid the pounding music and burning pain, I found a sense of calm, a clarity of mind that helped me focus on the task at hand. My muscles screamed in protest, but I moved to my punching bag, taking out my frustrations on an invisible enemy. The weight of the responsibility on my shoulders felt lighter, the fear less overwhelming. With each blow, each lift, I pushed at the darkness that threatened to consume me.

When the last note of the song I was listening to faded, however, and I collapsed onto the mat gasping for breath, the tension in my chest found its way back to me, demanding my attention.

Heading into the shower, I stood beneath the spray, allowing the water to wash away the remnants of the intense workout, but it did nothing for the anxiety that had sent me there. All I could think about was Caroline. I didn't understand why she was avoiding me, what I had done to push her so far away. The way her eyes danced when she laughed, the scent of that damn floral shampoo...everything about her consumed my thoughts. Visions of her standing above me at the mountain lookout point as I licked her pussy had my cock hard enough to break glass. I needed her.

Wrapping my hand around my length, I stroked it hard, groaning at how good it felt. I allowed images of her to flood into my mind, her curves, her breathy sighs, the way she arched her back when she climaxed. The thought of being inside her, feeling her body tremble around me, sent a surge of desire through me that I knew my hand would never satisfy, but I needed the release.

I braced myself on the cold tile and stroked harder, a moan escaping my lips. The pressure built within me, the memory of her becoming more vivid with each passing second. My hand moved faster and harder, the tension in my balls growing more intense. I closed my eyes, reliving the moment when we were first together, the raw passion and connection we shared.

And then the dam broke. Shuddering with a groan, the pent-up energy flowed out of me. As the euphoria washed over me, I leaned against the wall, trying to catch my breath, fighting to erase Caroline from my mind, but it was useless. I had a purpose, something worth fighting for, and when all was said and done and she and her family were safe, I had every intention of getting her back.

CHAPTER 20
The Phoenix

The silence of the early morning was shattered by the blaring of my alarm clock. Scarlett had an early morning doctor's appointment and Ethan went with her, so I had to open the bookstore by myself. We had a few other employees, but none who could come in for opening duties. Groaning and rolling over, I slapped the snooze button in a futile attempt to steal a few more precious minutes of sleep. Beside me, Evie lay curled up under the covers, her little chest rising and falling with each breath. My little fighter. She'd been feeling sick ever since her chemotherapy the day before, so I'd let her sleep with me.

As I lay there watching her sleep, the events of two days ago came rushing back—the way Tristan and I had left things, and the hurt in his eyes as he'd walked away. The more I dwelled on it, the more I regretted the cold way in which I'd treated him, how I'd let fear get the better of me and cloud my judgment. He deserved better. We both did, but I didn't know how to make it right, so I was stuck in some sort of holding pattern as I waited for the courage to say I was sorry.

Love terrified me, its loss too painful to endure again. But the longing in my heart remained—the way he made me feel only made it more pronounced. I craved the joy and comfort love could bring. The passion I once knew, the passion I'd only glimpsed when I shared a night with Tristan. He made me feel alive again, and didn't I deserve that?

A soft moan drew me back. Evie stirred, her face pale.

"How are you feeling, nugget?"

"My tummy hurts," she whimpered, snuggling closer into my side.

I pressed my hand to her forehead, grateful there was no fever, just the chemo roiling her insides.

"Maybe you should stay home today," I said, sliding my thumb across her soft cheek. "I'll need to bring you to work with me this morning, but as soon as Aunt Scarlett and Uncle Ethan get back from the doctor, we'll have a mommy-daughter day, just you and me."

Her eyes lit up at that. My brave girl. Although she'd endured so much more than a child ever should, her spirit remained unbroken. I only wished I could be the same.

After getting Evie dressed and medicated, I loaded her into the car and headed to the bookstore. She curled up in the backseat, clutching her stuffed llama in one hand and the new unicorn in the other, her nausea temporarily abated.

Once at the store, I busied myself with opening tasks while Evie played in the children's section. The familiar routine of preparing the bookstore and cafe for the day provided a sense of normalcy amidst the chaos of my thoughts. Moving behind the counter, I switched on the register, counting the till and checking the receipts from the day before. When that was done, I went into the cafe part of the store and started brewing a fresh pot of coffee.

Glancing at the clock after moving around the store to make sure everything was in place, I realized it was almost time to unlock the doors, so I picked up the pace, not used to opening by myself. With a few minutes remaining, I walked to the children's section to find Evie sitting on the ground playing with the toy train, completely content. I gave her a kiss on the head and then went back to the front.

Unlocking the door and turning on the open sign, I returned behind the counter to check on the coffee and set out the pastries for the day. The bell above the door chimed while my back was turned, but my heart fell into my stomach when I turned and took in the appearances of the two men who'd entered the store. With their dark hats and faces obscured by sunglasses, I couldn't make out much of their features. Still, something about their demeanor set off warning bells in my mind. Instinctively, I glanced toward the children's section, relief flooding me when I didn't see Evie out in the open. There was something about them that filled me with fear, and all I could think of was that I wished she'd gone to school.

Pasting a smile across my face, I tried to keep my voice steady. "Good morning. How can I help you gentlemen?"

One of them stepped forward, a gleam of metal reflecting the sunlight inside his pocket—a gun. He had a gun. "Scarlett, we need to have a word with you."

Scarlett? I could see where they might have been confused. We both worked in the bookstore, were only two years apart, and both had a similar hair color. But if they didn't know her well enough to know that I wasn't my sister-in-law, that meant the situation I found myself in could be dangerous. Still, I couldn't bring myself to correct him. The only thought flashing through my mind was to do whatever they said so they wouldn't harm my daughter, and so they wouldn't stay in the store until Scarlett arrived and hurt her too.

Swallowing back the burning dread in my throat, I nodded. "Is there something I can help you with, gentlemen?"

Before I could move away, the taller of the two men closed the distance between us and grabbed my arm in a bruising grip, catching me by surprise. The cold barrel of the gun pushed into my side as he pulled me against his body. "I know there's a child somewhere in this store with you, so I suggest you remain silent if you want us to leave her alive."

Icy fear and panic numbed my limbs, but I managed to nod, my eyes darting toward the back of the store again to make sure Evie hadn't emerged to see what was happening. "Please don't hurt her. I'll do whatever you want me to... Just please leave her alone."

"You're coming with us," he snarled, pushing the gun harder into my back. "Now."

With his massive hand wrapped around my bicep, he propelled me toward the door. My heels scraped against the pavement as they dragged me outside, the morning sun blinding me momentarily. Thoughts moved through my mind in a chaotic rush as I struggled to understand what was happening, and why it was happening to me.

Without another word, they yanked me toward the black SUV—the same black SUV I'd seen parked outside my house several times. The man on the left yanked open the rear door and shoved me inside, my shoulder landing hard on the opposite side of the vehicle as the door slammed behind me. Through the tinted windows, I watched the bookstore grow smaller in the distance as we drove away.

Once we were a few miles away from the bookstore, the man riding shotgun twisted around to face me, his eyes invisible behind dark lenses. From what I could tell, he was middle-aged, his dirty blond hair turning gray. He still held his gun in his hand, as though I was stupid enough to try and fight him completely unarmed in a moving vehicle.

"You must have caused someone a lot of trouble for the hefty bounty payout they offered to whoever could bring you in." Taking a slow look at me from head to toe, his lips twisted, and he reached forward to slide the barrel of the gun up the inside of my thigh. I jerked away, tears burning the backs of my eyes as he reached forward and grabbed my thigh to hold me in place. "Calm down, little girl. I was just admiring the goods. I can see why the high dollar if they plan on selling you at auction. Those thighs on you just beg to be wrapped around a man's waist, perfect for making babies. You would bring in a high price, indeed."

Panic clawed at my throat, my mind looking for a way out even while I saw none. No matter what it took, if they were planning on selling me, I had to find a way out of it—any way out.

The SUV sped through the streets, weaving in and out of traffic with reckless abandon. To my relief, the passenger had turned back around in his seat, my captors remaining silent and ignoring my presence in the backseat. I kept my eyes fixed out the window, watching for any landmarks that might tell me where we were headed, but the man in the passenger seat noticed and turned back around before climbing over the center console and dropping into the seat beside me. Before I could even think of what he intended to do to me, he pulled a black cloth out of his pocket, pressing it to my face. I flinched as a cloying chemical scent filled my nostrils. I pushed against his hold, but it was no use. As darkness seeped into the edges of my mind, my last thoughts were of Evie. I prayed she had called Ethan or 911. I had to stay alive for my little girl, no matter what these men had planned.

When I came to, my head throbbed. A blindfold covered my eyes, preventing me from seeing anything, and my hands were bound behind my back. Panic set in, making the air too thin as my lungs tried to take in enough oxygen to keep me conscious. The vehicle stopped. A moment later, doors slammed as the men got out, then wrenched me from the backseat. I stumbled along in their hold, faint sounds of gravel crunching under our footsteps.

A heavy metal door creaked open, and we entered a musty, cold space. My footsteps echoed off concrete walls and bare walls, the scent of dust in the air making me sneeze.

Shoving me down into a chair, one of the men removed my blindfold. I blinked against the harsh fluorescent lights of what looked like an abandoned warehouse. Dust motes danced in the beams from the dingy windows near the ceiling.

A separate set of men stood before me, one with long black hair pulled back in a low ponytail, mid forties, and the other an older man, his gray hair balding in the center. Behind them, two younger men stood guard, assault rifles in their hands as they watched me.

The man with the long hair stepped forward and grasped my jaw, his face inches from mine.

"Where's your father being kept, Scarlett? Tell me where to find Ivy, and we might just let you go."

I met his glare, forcing a strength into my voice that I did not feel. "I told your men in the car that I don't know what any of this is about. I do not know where Ivy is."

He sneered. "Have it your way. I'm not a patient man, but we've got a little time to jog your memory."

Turning on his heel, he followed the other man out the door, a heavy lock clicking behind them, and then I was alone, still secured to the chair. I tested the ropes, but they held fast. I was trapped—for now.

Knowing panicking wouldn't help, I took a deep breath, trying to center myself. I needed to stay calm and assess the situation.

Glancing around, I spotted a grimy window about fifteen feet up on the wall to my left. If I could get free and reach it, I realized it may be my only way out, but I had to be smart and patient—make them underestimate me.

With nowhere to go, my thoughts turned to Evie, scared and alone back at the bookstore. At least she was safe for the moment, though no doubt terrified about what happened to me. I wondered if Scarlett and Ethan had gone to the bookstore yet to find her there alone. And Tristan... Once he knew I was gone, he would be frantic and would use all his technical skills to track me down. I wished I could reach out to them and let them both know I was alright for now, that I would not give up. That was the moment when I remembered the tracking divide still clipped to the band of my watch, but my hands were bound behind my back. I pulled on the ropes again, but there was no give.

Footsteps approached and I steeled myself, needing to be strong for my family.

The door opened and the long-haired man entered alone, cracking his knuckles. A pistol was holstered at his hip and a dagger around his thigh. I realized it was time for me to put on an act. If I was meek and compliant, maybe they would at least unbind my hands. I needed the use of them to have any chance at escape.

"Ready to talk?" he asked, straddling the chair in front of me.

I dropped my gaze. "Please. I don't know anything. Just let me go back to my family."

Hand shooting up, he grabbed my chin, forcing me to look at him. "Nice try, but we're just getting started."

I took a shaky breath as he released my chin and began pacing around me. "Why are you doing this?" I asked, my voice quivering. "I'm not sure what I'm supposed to tell you. I don't know where Ivy is."

He let out a humorous chuckle, turning back to face me. "Come on, we're not idiots. We know you're Ivy Etienne's daughter, so you must know something about where he's being kept. Just tell us where he is, and this will all be over."

Widening my eyes in faux confusion, I shook my head. "I'm telling you, you have the wrong person. My name is Amy. I do not know who Ivy is or where he is."

A burst of pain shot through my face as he backhanded me, several teeth tearing into the inside of my cheek and filling my mouth with blood.

"Wrong answer. I'm done playing nicely. You're going to tell me everything you know about the Etienne organization and the deal he has with the FBI, or you won't be leaving this room."

Defeated, I slumped forward, pulling on the ropes binding my wrists. "Please, let me go. I'm just a single mom working to pay for my child's medical treatments. I don't know anything about any organization."

Grabbing a handful of my hair, he yanked my head back. I cried out as he pressed a knife to my throat, the blade stinging as it grazed my skin. "Last chance. Give me what I want, or you die right here."

CHAPTER 21

The Survivor

The bookstore was eerily silent when we returned after my obstetrician appointment, sending an icy chill down my spine. Although the store should have been open, the lights were all off and the front door was locked. I'd received a text from Caroline that morning, so I knew she was supposed to be at work, but it was clear she wasn't there anymore.

"This is strange," I said, my eyes meeting Ethan's worried glance. "Caroline was supposed to cover the store this morning."

Before Ethan could respond, a tiny figure ran toward the glass door from the inside of the store, her face red from crying.

"Oh my gosh. Unlock the door. Hurry!" Visibly trembling, Ethan placed the key in the latch, Evie's muffled sobs reaching our ears from across the panel. The moment we stepped inside, she dropped to the ground, cheeks stained with tears, little body shaking.

"Where's your mommy, munchkin?" Ethan said, crouching down beside me as I gathered her in my arms. She clung to me, face buried in my shoulder. Over her head, I couldn't miss the terror and utter confusion on Ethan's face.

"Shh, it's okay," I soothed, stroking her bald head. "We're here now, sweetheart. Where's your mommy?"

Sniffling, Evie pulled away enough to look into my eyes. "The bad men. The bad men took Mommy."

Beside me, Ethan's jaw tightened, eyes darkening like a gathering storm as he headed for the office where the cameras were. I knew that look because I'd seen it before, and it only sank my heart more. He was preparing for war, ready to move heaven and earth to bring Caroline home.

Gently, I lifted Evie's chin, looking into her puffy, red-rimmed eyes. "Uncle Ethan and I won't let anything happen to her. We'll bring her back to you."

Evie sniffled again, her lower lip trembling. "You promise?"

Even though it was a promise I didn't know I could keep, I nodded, heart aching for her. "I promise, sweet girl."

Jaw tightening, Ethan pulled out his phone, dialing a number as he paced. "Tristan," he said gruffly when the call connected. "I need you to trace the traffic cameras near the bookstore for a black SUV. Now. Caroline's gone. She was taken from the bookstore this morning. We got back from the doctor and found Evie alone."

I rubbed Evie's back as she clung to me, her small body tense.

"No, but I'm sure they are just in it for the bounties. They probably don't know anything about her. I need you to run facial recognition. See if anything picks up. And get on the traffic cams. We need to find that SUV." Ethan continued, his tone brooking no argument. "But Phantom, I need you here as soon as you can get here. I need to look for Caroline, but I can't leave Scarlett and Evie home alone, even with the safe room."

The thought of my husband—the man who was my entire world, who'd saved me in more ways than one, and who was the father of my child—returning to that life where he may never make it back home sickened me to the point where I thought I would vomit, but I pushed it down. This was Caroline, and she needed to be rescued. There was no other option.

Still on the phone, Ethan nodded, though Tristan clearly couldn't see him through the phone. "If you trust him with your life and my sister's, then put him on the cameras and you get on your way down here. Call me when you're close or if you get any information while on your way, so I can prepare."

Ending the call, he met my eyes, his jaw set. "Tristan is putting his mentor on the cameras so he can get on the road. We'll find her."

I nodded, trusting in Ethan's instincts. Lifting Evie into my arms, I followed Ethan out to our SUV, securing her with the seatbelt.

As we drove back home, my hand found Ethan's, squeezing tightly. He brought our joined hands to his lips, pressing a fierce kiss to my knuckles.

"I'll bring her home, Little Red. I'm going to bring her home and end this once and for all."

Once we turned onto the road that led up the mountain to our property, Ethan drove with laser focus, his grip tight on the steering wheel. The tension in his shoulders was unmistakable, the barely restrained fury simmering beneath the surface.

Our new home in the mountains was supposed to be our sanctuary. It was the reason we'd moved there, but suddenly nowhere felt safe. This time, when we reached the cabin and he checked the remote cameras from his phone before ushering Evie and I quickly inside and locking the door behind us, I was reminded of the time he and I hid out in the cabin further south as we hid from my ex-husband. Just the thought of everything we'd gone through only sickened me more. I could not believe we were going through this again.

The safe room was in the basement, accessible only by a hidden door and passcode that Ethan swiftly keyed in. Inside, the space was like a small apartment, prepared for exactly this purpose—stocked with non-perishable food, water, blankets, and basic medical supplies, including a backup supply of any medications we needed, including those that Evie took. There was a bedroom area on one side as well as a small bathroom. In the corner was a children's area where we'd set up a small bed, toys, and a bassinet for when the baby came. Whether for a storm, or a home invasion, we were set up to survive below for months if we had to. Some would have seen our preparations as overkill, but after what we'd survived together, it was what we needed to feel safe. It was what I needed.

Stepping into the space, I settled Evie on her little bed with her stuffed animals, wrapping a blanket around her shoulders.

"It's okay, sweetie," I said, squeezing her hand. "You're safe here. Uncle Ethan is going to bring your mommy back soon. Are you hungry?"

As I stood up to make her a snack, Ethan crouched down beside her, brushing a hand over her head. "I promise, munchkin. I'm going to go find your mommy, so you'll need to stay here with your Auntie Scarlett."

He pressed a gentle kiss to her forehead before rising and crossing the space to me. Cradling my face in his hands, his thumbs brushed over my cheeks, and he leaned in to kiss me.

"I have to get ready, *mon joli petit aman*t," he said, regret lacing his tone. "Tristan will be here soon. Don't open the door for anyone but him."

I nodded, leaning into his touch, the muscles of my chest squeezing uncomfortably. "Just come back to us—both of you. *Please.*"

Eyes softening, he leaned down and kissed me hard, lingering against my lips a moment longer as his hand slid up to touch my belly, where his daughter was safely growing inside me. "I'll always come back to you, Little Red."

With one last glance, the love of my life slipped out the door, locking it securely behind him. For a long moment, I stared at the solid piece of metal, wrapping my arms around myself, and hoping we'd all make it through this nightmare.

CHAPTER 22
The Phantom

The shrill ring of my phone pierced the silence of my apartment, jolting me from my work. Ethan didn't even wait until I greeted him before he spoke.

"Tristan. I need you to track the traffic cameras near the bookstore for a black SUV. Now. Caroline's gone. She was taken from the bookstore this morning. We got back from the doctor and found Evie alone."

Ice flooded my veins, my greatest fears coming to fruition, forcing bile up my esophagus. Caroline had been so sure that a black SUV parked on her street was watching her, but then she'd started to question herself, thinking she was being paranoid. It turned out she'd been right the entire time, and I'd left her and Evie alone in that house only two days ago. I'd left them in danger, running away like a coward.

"And you don't recognize them at all? The two men?"

The sound of Evie crying met my ears through the phone line, shredding my heart into pieces.

"No, but I'm sure they are just in it for the bounties. They probably don't know anything about her. I need you to run facial recognition. See if anything picks up. And get on the traffic cams. We need to find that SUV." He went quiet for a moment, and I could barely pick up the sound of Scarlett talking in the background. When he came back, his tone was even sharper. "But Phantom, I need you here as soon as you can get here. I need to look for Caroline, but I can't leave Scarlett and Evie home alone, even with the safe room."

My fingers trembled, yearning to spring into action, to scour every pixel of footage until I found her, but this was too big for me alone, especially if I needed to drive back to Alabama.

"I'll call Legacy," I said, my mentor's weathered face flashing in my mind. "He picked me up off the streets when I was a kid and taught me everything I know. We can trust him. He can access the feeds faster, so I can head your way."

Although Ethan always wanted to keep his circle as small as possible, he grunted in agreement, desperation seeping into his usual stoicism. We both knew that we needed help if we were going to find her. "If you trust him with your life and my sister's, then put him on the cameras and you get on your way down here. Call me when you're close or if you get any information while on your way, so I can prepare."

Ending the call moments later, Caroline's name pounded through me with each rapid heartbeat, making it impossible to focus on what I needed to do next. My hands shook as I grabbed my phone again, quickly dialing into Legacy's secure line as I pulled up the link for the GPS device I'd given to Caroline, slamming my hand down on the desk when it showed no signal. Wherever she was, it wasn't sensing her. All I could hope was that she had it on her and they hadn't found it yet, so that maybe it would pick up a signal eventually. It was the one thing that could help us find her immediately, if the signal ever went through.

As I stood from my desk and started shoving clothing and equipment into multiple duffle bags, Legacy answered, his gravelly voice grounding me. I did my best to explain the situation, my words spilling out in a jumbled mess, but he didn't hesitate.

"Consider it done," he said, warmth lacing his tone. "Go to them. I'll be in touch."

I whispered thanks, the relief washing over me allowing me to put one foot in front of the other so I could pack my car and get on the road. Placing Houdini in his carrier, I grabbed the last few items I needed, double checking my bags before making my first trip to the parking garage. With the litter box and all my equipment, it took three trips for me to finally get everything loaded. But once it was, I wasted no time gripping the wheel and pulling out into the afternoon sun.

Storm clouds moved in as I drove, the countryside and eventually the mountains flying past in a blur, but my mind was far away, lost in a chaotic blend of anger at myself and fear for Caroline. I thought back to the first real conversation Caroline, and I had in her car, when she'd told me about her life before Alabama—when her fierce resilience and fiery spirit drew me in despite my best efforts to remain detached. She saw right through my loner facade to the real me hidden underneath. She seemed to see me in a way no one else ever had. We hadn't had much time together, but it was enough to know that if she'd wanted to, she could have wrapped her tiny hands around my heart and held it forever.

Other stolen moments flashed through my mind—her smile that made my heart skip a beat; the brush of her hand against mine that sent sparks skittering across my skin; our day at the park where we slid down the slide a hundred times with Evie, laughing our asses off; her vulnerability and passion when she opened herself up to me intimately, holding nothing back until the guilt from her loss set in and stole her joy. It stole her away from me.

In such a brief time, she had become something akin to my compass, what I'd always seen as home circling until it pointed directly at her. And now that she was lost, I felt adrift, torn from my moorings, an anchorless ship cast out into a raging sea.

My hands tightened on the wheel as I pictured her bound and frightened, crying out for help. No matter how conflicted her emotions had become, I should have done more to protect her. I should have kept her safe. And if something would have happened to Evie... That was a realistic possibility I couldn't face. A storm raged through my blood, getting more violent with every mile.

The winding mountain road stretched on endlessly before me as I pressed my foot down on the gas pedal, urging my car to go faster. My fingers gripped the steering wheel tightly, my knuckles white with tension. I replayed our last conversation in my mind, analyzing every word, every nuance, wishing I'd handled her rejection better. Heavy with regret, my chest ached, wishing I could tell her I was sorry.

Nestled amongst the towering pines and rugged mountains, Ethan and Scarlett's cabin came into view after two hours of driving in a panic. I had already spoken to Legacy twice, but he was still searching for the SUV, which had proven to be more difficult than I'd expected. To our dismay, they appeared to have stayed on rural roads, eluding the traffic cameras that resided along every big city street and highway. Her captors had become ghosts, but he was not giving up that easily, and as soon as I was set up in the safe room of the cabin, I would join him in the search.

Relief washed over me as I pulled into the cabin's driveway and killed the engine, noticing Ethan's dark silhouette lingering on the porch. He closed the distance between us before I had even pulled all my gear out of the car.

"Any leads on Caroline?" he asked, keeping in step at my side.

I shook my head, wishing I had better news to share. "Legacy is working on it, but they appear to have taken backroads after leaving town to the east."

Hands clenching into fists, he grabbed one of my bags, carrying it back toward the front door. "I need you to dig, deep as you can. Find anything to give us direction."

I nodded, stopping by the front door to set Houdini's carrier down before heading back to the car to grab the rest of my stuff. "I'm on it, boss. I'll set up in the surveillance room downstairs, get a dedicated connection running." Reaching forward, I set a hand on his shoulder, not knowing how much I wanted to reveal, but wanting him to understand how invested I was. "I care deeply for Caroline, so the stakes are just as high for me. We'll find her, boss. We must."

Dipping his chin, he dismissed me to go inside and set up, and we parted ways. There was so much more I wanted to say, but time was wasting, and we both had jobs to do if we were going to get Caroline back.

Stepping inside the cabin, the familiar scent of pine and a fragrance I could not quite place but that came from one of Scarlett's scented candles washed over me. It was a small comfort amidst the chaos. With Houdini in one hand, and bags in the other, I stepped into the master bedroom, opening the hidden door, and descending the stairs toward the reinforced safe room. I paused outside the heavy steel door, setting Houdini's carrier down and steadying myself before ringing the intercom.

"It's Tristan."

Within a mere breath, locks clicked, and the door swung open, and suddenly my arms were full of a tiny body. Evie crashed into me, her small frame trembling. Wrapping her in a tight hug, I lifted her off the ground, my heart aching. She had been through so much already, and now this. When we found Caroline, I intended to take care of them both, do anything I could to be a part of their family and make their lives easier.

Over her shoulder, I met Scarlett's worried gaze, her eyes bloodshot from crying. She looked pale but composed, her inner strength just as iron clad as the child in my arms.

"Hey, kiddo," I said, rubbing Evie's back. "I'm here now. We're going to get your mom back. I promise."

She sniffled against my shirt, her tiny arms wrapping tighter around my neck. "I want my mommy."

"I know. We all do." For the next few minutes, I continued to hold her, waiting for her trembling to subside. Once the sniffles dried up, I extricated myself and crouched down to her level.

"Why don't you and your Auntie Scarlett get comfy in here and help set up Houdini's food and water while I set up my equipment so I can help Uncle Ethan look for Mommy?"

Evie nodded, only then noticing the black cat in the carrier beside me, which brought a small smile to her face. While Evie grabbed Houdini's carrier and dragged it through the doorway, Scarlett stepped forward and wrapped me in a hug.

"We have to find her," she whispered against my chest.

I nodded, returning the hug just as tightly. "I will. Whatever it takes."

With Evie and Scarlett stepping back into the safe room, I headed upstairs to gather the rest of my gear, and then went back outside to move my car into the barn on the far corner of the property, not far from the tunnel that led out of the safe space.

Once my car was out of sight, I jogged back to the house and set all the security systems to their highest setting before returning to the basement. From the outside, as well as from the inside, it would appear as though the house was empty—not that anyone should have had any reason to travel all the way up the winding mountain road, unless they were looking for trouble.

There was already a large sofa in the surveillance room, so I made that my space, bringing all my equipment inside with the intention to sleep in there, if I slept at all. While Scarlett moved around the small kitchen area as she made dinner and tended to Evie, I began setting up my equipment, muscle memory taking over as I connected my laptop and an array of tech to what we had already installed only days earlier, and powering everything on that wasn't. The familiar routine soothed me, bringing a sense of control. Once everything was powered on, I sank into the desk chair and cracked my knuckles, opening a secure connection to Legacy, hoping he had an update for me.

CHAPTER 23
The Savior

Alone in the hallway, I took a deep steadying breath. My hands curled into fists at my sides as I steeled my nerves for the fight ahead. I had been in countless dangerous situations before, but this time felt different. More was at stake now—not just my life, but Scarlett's, Evie's, Caroline's...my unborn daughter's.

Failure was not an option.

After pulling on my black hoodie, cargo pants, and combat boots, I retreated to the weapons room that was separate from the safe room, gearing up methodically as muscle memory took over: bulletproof vest first, then the twin hip and thigh holsters, sheathed knives, and extra ammo. I strapped a SIG Sauer P226 to my right thigh and a Glock 19 to my left. More firepower waited in the duffel bag. I preferred to kill with a blade, but it was always a bad idea to bring a knife to a gunfight. My favorite knife was sheathed at my thigh, so I was not leaving home without it, but I needed to be prepared for anything.

Satisfied with my arsenal, I sank down onto a stool and dropped my head into my hands. Doubt and anger warred within me, guilt overpowering them both. I should have done more to protect my sister. Even with all the new security additions and wiping our identities everywhere I could, she had still fallen into a dangerous situation that she didn't belong in. How could I have let this happen?

My phone vibrated in my pocket, breaking my spiraling thoughts. Tristan was not far. With one final look back at the door to the safe room, I closed the door to our bedroom and headed outside.

Tristan's Mustang came down the driveway just as I stepped onto the front porch. When he stepped out of the car, a cat carrier in one hand and a duffle bag in the other, his face was grim, jaw clenched.

"Any leads on Caroline?" I asked before he even reached me.

The shaking of his head sent my stomach tumbling. "Legacy is working on it, but they appear to have taken backroads after leaving town to the west."

My hands clenched into fists, but I refrained from looking for something to punch. Adrenaline surged so forcefully beneath my skin that I needed to do something quickly or that could change. "I need you to dig, deep as you can. Find anything to give us direction."

Tristan nodded, determination flashing behind his glasses. "I'm on it, boss. I'll set up in the surveillance room downstairs, get a dedicated connection running." Eyes softening, he clasped my shoulder. "I care deeply for Caroline, so the stakes are just as high for me. We'll find her, boss. We must."

All I managed was a tight smile in return. Tristan's skills were unmatched—if anyone could track her down, it was him.

Alone on the porch, I breathed in the fresh mountain air as the peacefulness of my surroundings belied what lay ahead. Things were about to get bloody, because for Caroline, I would tear through anyone who stood in my way.

With one last look at my home, I headed to the barn and slid behind the wheel of my black Lexus, the need to hunt heating my blood. My knuckles tightened around the steering wheel as I pulled onto the road, heading for New Orleans, since I did not know where else they could have taken her. Caroline was counting on me, and I would not fail her. Not again. Never again.

The highway stretched endlessly into the late evening as I drove toward New Orleans, my grip white-knuckled on the steering wheel. Caroline was out there somewhere, her fate unknown, and the not knowing ate away at me.

I thought back to how we had grown up together, two kids against the world. We only had each other for the longest time. Survivors of a brutal world that had little kindness for the weak or wayward. But we persevered, hardened by the flames that had once engulfed our lives after engulfing our parents' car when we were teens. From the ashes we rose, and there was nothing I would not do to protect her.

A deep ache twisted in my chest at the thought of what she might have been going through. Caroline was strong, but she had already been through so much, and everyone had a breaking point. If Victor's men had taken her, it was surely to be used as leverage against Scarlett and her father. The thought made my blood boil.

This was all because of *my* past—Scarlett's past. Caroline did not deserve to get caught up in the wreckage, innocent Evie either. They were the best parts of my life, untainted by the darkness that had taken over so much. I had always shielded them from it, but they got pulled into it anyway. The farther I drove into the darkening sky, the more fear and rage entwined, twisting into a molten core of steel in my belly. I would not fail. I could not afford weakness, not now when so much was at stake: Caroline's life. My family's safety. The security I had fought tooth and nail to build, now crumbling around me.

I pressed down on the accelerator, urging my car to go faster. After hours of driving, streetlights streaked by as I sped toward the city limits, toward the safe house I had used many times before, jaw clenched. New Orleans had taken so much from me already. I would not let it take Caroline too. They would pay for even trying. There would be no mercy, no escape for the monsters that had started this war.

The beast inside me stirred, snarling in fury after being locked away for so long. It strained against its chains, waiting to be unleashed. Let them come, it said. Let them come and I will tear them all apart for touching my family.

CHAPTER 24

The Phoenix

Frigid cold seeped into my bones, stirring me from unconsciousness. My head pounded as I blinked, trying to clear the fog from my vision and figure out where in the hell I was.

Groaning, I shifted on the hard concrete floor, every muscle in my body screaming in protest. Memories of what happened to me before everything had gone black came flooding back into my mind like the blows the long-haired mobster had rained down on me. Now I found myself in the same barren room, empty except for a dirty mattress in the corner, a bucket, and a chair. At least I was no longer tied to it.

Slowly I sat up, squinting against the dim light filtering through the small window high on the opposite wall. All I could see through the dusty glass was a swath of gray sky, the tips of evergreen trees, and mountains rising in the distance. We were somewhere remote. Somewhere no one would find me.

Fear slithered down my spine like a serpent as I stared at the knob less door. There was no way out. I was trapped at the mercy of vicious men who thought I was someone else—someone who they thought had the information they wanted. Although I was not Scarlett, I knew she did not know where her father was. And although I was not Scarlett, I was relieved that I had been taken instead of her, because I had a feeling that her pregnancy wouldn't have stopped them from hurting her and killing her baby.

Thoughts of my family sent a shiver through me, the cold seeping into my soul. Would I ever see Evie's smiling face again? Hear her sweet laugh? And my brother, he was undoubtedly frantic with worry, picking up the sword he'd finally locked away for the chance at a normal life, and now this would drag him right back into the darkness—the darkness where I wasn't sure his wife would want to follow, not with a new baby on the way. The lump of dread in my throat was almost too constricting to swallow around, realizing my family might be lost to me forever.

Dragging myself upright, I limped to the window on an ankle I'd somehow twisted, pain shooting through my leg as I stood on the tips of my toes to gauge the distance, but it was just too high. There was a possibility I would be able to look out if I stood on the chair, but bolts held it to the floor. Even if I could reach the window, it was too small, at least from what I could tell. I needed to find a way out of the nightmare I found myself in and back to my family, but the window did not appear to be it.

Blowing out a breath that sent pain through my ribs, I turned away from the small window, my gaze landing on a sandwich and a cup of water sitting beside the mattress. My stomach rumbled, reminding me I had not eaten in who knew how long. Part of me recoiled at the idea of accepting anything from my captors, but I knew I needed to keep up my strength if I hoped to escape.

Reluctantly, I dropped onto the lumpy mattress and picked up the plate, taking a small bite of the sandwich. My jaw ached as I chewed—no doubt bruised from the beating that knocked me out, and my mouth still tasted like copper from the gashes on the inside of my cheek. Although the bread tasted stale, I forced myself to eat every last crumb, forcing it down with a gulp of water. I needed nourishment.

As I sat on the mattress, head still pounding, heavy foot-steps echoed down the hallway. My pulse quickened, dread pooling in my gut and threatening to send the food I had eaten back up and onto the floor. I had only seen him a few times, but I recognized the footfalls of the long-haired man who'd slammed his fist into my face when I couldn't give him the answers he wanted. Maybe he was coming to fulfill his earlier threats, but I could not find the energy to cower in the corner. I could not find the energy to move at all.

The scrape of a key in a lock echoed through the nearly silent building, and the door creaked open. He strode in, flanked by the same two, armed men who'd come with him before, his long hair secured back with a band, every piece of clothing on his body black. His cold eyes bored into me as his mouth curled into a malicious smile that sent ice through my veins.

"Ready to talk now, Scarlett?" he growled, taking a step closer to me, stopping a few feet away.

I instinctively scooted back, my hands trembling as I met his cruel stare. "I've told you, my name is Amy. I don't know anything about Scarlett or Ivy Etienne."

Crossing the room in two quick strides, he grabbed a fistful of my hair, forcing a cry from my throat as he yanked my head back.

"Lying won't save you now, little bitch," he hissed in my ear, his breath reeking of cigarette smoke. Tears burned the backs of my eyes, but I forced them to hold off, at least until I was alone. "You'll tell me where your father is, or I will kill you. My patience is running thin."

Fear and defiance warred within me, twisting my chest into knots. I wanted to beg for mercy, to beg for my life, but I could not betray Scarlett. I could not lead these monsters back to her. So, I held silent, blinking back my tears, and bracing myself for what was to come.

Face twisting with fury, his fingers wrapped tighter in my hair, wrenching another whimper from my throat as the strands popped.

"Last chance," he snarled. "Where is Ivy Etienne?"

I squeezed my eyes shut, willing myself not to break, afraid of what he would do next. "I told you, I don't know any Ivy Etienne. I would tell you if I did."

With a roar of rage, he slammed my head against the concrete wall. Pain exploded through my skull and stars burst across my vision. I slumped forward, head spinning as the tears finally fell.

Grabbing my chin, he forced me to meet his eyes. The eyes looking back at me were no longer human, if they ever had been. It was a wild animal staring back at me—feral—and only moments away from foaming at the mouth. "You think you can hold out on me? I'll beat the truth out of you if I have to."

He drew back his fist and I flinched, bracing for another blow, but before he swung, the door banged open again, another armed man stepping into the room.

"The boss wants to see you," he said gruffly, seeming unphased by the scene before him. They were all monsters. "Says it can't wait."

Cursing under his breath, my attacker released me and stepped toward the door. The moment his strength was no longer holding me upright, I sagged against the wall, relief washing over me, but my reprieve was short-lived as he turned to look over his shoulder. "Don't go anywhere. We're not finished with our little chat."

Twisting back around, he stepped out of the room, the door slamming shut behind him with an ominous finality. I was alone again, but I knew it was only a matter of time before my torment resumed—a torment that I was starting to realize I may not survive.

The energy draining out of me with the drops of blood trailing down my face, I slumped against the concrete wall, wincing as my bruised body protested the movement. I forced my breathing to slow, trying to calm my pounding heart, but everything hurt, making it difficult to breathe at all.

My thoughts drifted to my daughter, her smiling face appearing in my mind's eye, her eyes bright with the joy she always exuded, even when life was too hard. She would be so heartbroken if something happened to me, but I knew Ethan and Scarlett would take care of her. I was certain of that. He loved Evie as if she were his own. If I did not make it back home, they would look after each other. The thought gave me some comfort even as tears pricked my eyes. I never meant to leave Evie so soon after our time together had just returned to some semblance of normalcy, but in the bleak circumstances I found myself in, escape seemed impossible. All I could do was hope my brother found me before it was too late.

Unable to shield my mind from my heart, I thought of Tristan, with his shy smile and those intense hazel eyes that seemed to look right through me. We had only shared one night of passion together before I'd pushed him away, too wrapped up in my own grief to let him in. The realization that I might never get the chance to make things right tore at the fragile threads keeping my heart together.

Regret washed over me, breaking the wound in my chest wide open. After losing so much with Daniel, I had thought that staying away from love was the best way to protect myself, but I'd been fooling myself all along. I should not have been so cold to Tristan, not when warmth and affection were what I really craved deep down. After three years of grief and loneliness, I needed to allow others back in, and if by some miracle I got out of this, I would not make that mistake again. I promised myself that if I made it out alive, I would tell Tristan how I felt—that I wanted to explore the spark between us. For the moment, that hope gave me the strength to cling to life a little longer.

As I allowed myself to spiral, voices met my ears from the other side of the door, but the key did not jingle in the lock. Holding my breath for a moment, I waited for someone to enter, but when they did not, I crawled closer to the door, pressing my ear against the cool metal. With how swollen my face was, it felt good.

"It's her," one of the men said, his voice gruff as though he had been smoking for a lifetime. "It must be her. Same build...black hair. Bookstore. She's lying."

The other man scoffed, the same man who had been assaulting me. "If it is her, she's a lot closer to her father than sources claim. Either that, or she really doesn't have any insight on him, because she's risking her life to protect that piece of shit."

Both men went silent for a moment, before the heavy smoker spoke again. "So, what does the boss want to do? I don't think she's gonna talk. Not if she hasn't by now."

Adjusting my weight off my aching ankle, I sat on the ground, leaning back against the wall. I pressed my cheek against the door again just in time to hear the long-haired man clear his throat, his voice going lower as though he stepped farther away. "We can't let her go, so Aresco wants to list her. If she's lucky, her family will find her before the auction. Either way, he intends to get the money he's owed by her father."

Heart dropping into the concrete beneath me, I scurried to the back of the room, barely making it away from the door before everything in my stomach came hurling back up. He was going to sell me, auction me off like cattle to the highest bidder to make the money back that he had lost to Scarlett's father. I was out of time. I had to find a way out of the twisted game I was an unwilling participant in before I was sold and disappeared forever, leaving Evie without a mother and Ethan without a sister. Leaving Tristan...

With every ounce of strength I could muster, I stood, stumbling to the chair, and yanking hard, but it barely moved. Adrenaline coursed through me as I frantically scanned the room, the rate of my heartbeat, or possibly the concussion, making me sway. This time, when I yanked on the chair again, one of the screws bolting it into the floor popped, landing somewhere in the darkness. I blew out a breath, crouching to rest for a moment but wincing as I put too much pressure on my sore ankle.

For a few minutes, I just kneeled there, my head resting on my forearm as I held onto the chair, but I did not have the luxury of time.

Clenching my teeth, I rose back onto shaky legs, my hands white-knuckled on the chair as I put all I had into yanking it again.

Bolt ripping out of the floor, I toppled over, the chair landing on top of me when I hit the ground. I knew I had made too much noise, and the fear that one of them was still by the door and had heard me froze me in place. With no more air in my lungs, all I could do was lay there and try to breathe.

After I was sure no one was coming into the room, I rose back to my feet, pushing the chair and stumbling toward the window. My legs were weak, but I climbed onto the wobbly piece of furniture, holding onto the wall to peer out the window. Disappointment seized the breath in my lungs as I realized just how small the window was. Already broken on one side, the fresh mountain air came into the opening, taunting me with a freedom that I had no way to achieve. I would never be able to fit through the opening.

The tears barely came as I sucked in a breath, realizing how trapped I truly was, realizing the decision I would be forced to make if I did not want to end up on the auction block. If I could not get myself out, I would have to find a way to end my captivity on my own terms.

My hands shook as I fumbled to break a piece of glass off the already broken window, the jagged edge glinting under the dim light of the moon. Squeezing my eyes closed, I shook my head, the idea of leaving my family—my daughter—behind unbearable. But what awaited me if I lived? A life of cruelty, chained in some monster's basement. The light in my soul snuffed out. It would be a fate worse than death.

Reopening my eyes, I pressed the shard into my palm, wincing at the sharp sting. Beads of blood bubbled up and I watched them roll down my wrist, transfixed. My hand shook, the makeshift blade hovering over my wrist as I stared at the semicolon tattoo just above where I held the piece of glass. Just one quick slice down the veins. It would all be over. No more beatings, no auction block. No Ethan, or Evie, or future with Tristan.

I squeezed my eyes shut again, praying to the universe for courage. One breath in. One breath out. With a sob, I opened my eyes, tears clouding my vision, and yanked my watch off my wrist, the shard of glass dropping from my hand when a tiny black object the shape of a hair clip fell to the ground, it's smooth surface reflecting the light of the moon like a beacon to help me find my way home. *Tristan's tracking device.*

CHAPTER 25

The Phantom

The glare of the monitors seared my eyes as I scoured the dark web, chasing ghosts. What I really needed was sleep, but Caroline was out there somewhere, so I had to find her. There was no time for sleep, not until she was safe in her own bed.

My fingers moved across the keyboard, jumping from one encrypted site to the next. Dead ends and empty leads taunted me at every turn, an aching pit of failure in my chest growing bigger with every hour I did not find her.

As I searched through The Underbelly for more posts by ShadowRunner, a notification flashed on the bottom of my screen. I clicked it to find a grainy video clip waiting from Legacy. My mentor had been digging through surveillance footage since the day before looking for signs of the black SUV that was used in Caroline's abduction.

Pulled from the nearest city from where she had been taken, the new clip showed a black SUV with blacked-out windows cruising down a main thoroughfare before turning onto a side street. I held my breath as I ran the plates, but nothing pulled up in the system. It was likely the correct vehicle, but with no other camera footage to determine where they went from there, it was another dead end. Still, I forwarded the clip to Ethan.

Slamming my fist on the desk, the sting barely registered through the haze of desperation that clouded my mind. Caroline needed me to be at the top of my craft, but I had never felt so useless.

My fingers trembled as they returned to the keys, not knowing where to look next, when the door creaked open behind me, pulling me from the dark web's endless maze. I turned to see Evie's small frame silhouetted in the door-way, holding her stuffed llama in her hands.

"Hey, Captain," I said, opening my arms to her. She rushed over, burying her face in my chest. I stroked her head, wishing I could take away the pain and fear I knew raged inside her.

"Is my mommy going to be okay?" she asked, her voice quivering.

Squeezing my eyes shut, I hugged her tighter. "We're going to find her. I won't stop looking, no matter what it takes. Your mom is so strong and brave, so we just must be brave for her."

Evie nodded, her thin arms tightening around my neck.

We would find Caroline. We had to believe that, because I would not let Evie lose her mother, not after every-thing they'd survived together. Caroline's love and strength flowered through the child in my arms, so I had to keep going, for them both.

"Come on," I said, reaching for her hand. "Since Auntie Scarlett is sleeping, let me get you something to eat."

Taking my hand, Evie allowed me to lead her from the surveillance room, and into the small kitchen, fixing her a peanut butter and jelly sandwich. She picked at it silently, her eyes downcast and shoulders slumped.

For several minutes, I sat beside her, my own sandwich sitting on the table before me. I was so lost in thought that my phone buzzing in my pocket caused me to flinch. Standing and taking a few steps away from the table, I fished it out, my pulse quickening when I saw it was Ethan.

"Boss," I answered, my voice low. "Please tell me you have something."

"Maybe," he said, his voice sharp. "I'm heading to Marcel's now. I heard there were some out of towners there last night talking about a grab."

My grip on the phone tightened. "Do you think it's them? Could they have Caroline?"

Ethan sighed. "I don't know for sure, but I don't think she's here in the city. That camera footage you found—the SUV. If they were coming back to New Orleans, I don't know what they would have been doing on that stretch of road."

My mind raced. If she was not in New Orleans, she could be anywhere, but that also meant she could still be some-where in Alabama.

"I'll work on expanding the traffic cameras out—west and south," I said, already sending a message to Legacy. "Hopefully they didn't change vehicles on their way out of town."

"I can't even consider that possibility," he said, sounding a bit defeated. "I'm going to head to Marcel's, see if I can find out anything more. If there's no reason to suspect she's here, I'm heading back to you."

Glancing up at the clock, I shook my head. "She's been gone too long already."

I did not miss Ethan's sharp intake of breath. "I know. Watch over Evie and Scarlett and let me know if you find anything. I'll let you know when I am on my way back."

"I will."

Without saying goodbye, we hung up. I braced myself on the kitchen counter, exhaling slowly, doing my best to hide how worried I was from Evie. When I turned around, Scarlett was heading toward us, having just exited the bedroom. She had been sleeping for a few hours, but her eyes were still heavily shadowed from exhaustion.

"Hey," I said, setting the other plate of food I had made for Scarlett on the table and then lowering myself back into the chair. "I made sandwiches."

She gave me a knowing look, one that said she could see straight through my act. "We haven't heard anything new?"

I shook my head. "All we have so far is a grainy video with an SUV heading west. Ethan's still searching down south, but I have a feeling he'll be heading back this way soon. We are concerned that she may not be there at all."

If I were being honest, I was not sure who I was trying to convince more—her or myself.

For the next few minutes, I tried to force food into my stomach, watching as Scarlett and Evie did the same. Worry hung over us like a storm cloud, dampening even Evie's usual vibrant spirit. I hated watching her light dim.

Suddenly, a sharp chirp from the other room made us all jump, but I was out of my chair before I could explain what the sound meant. I dropped into the chair in front of the monitors within seconds, Scarlett and Evie running in behind me. I stared at the computer screen for a moment, hardly daring to believe what I was seeing. The tracking software had lit up with a notification.

"What is it?" Scarlett's panicked voice pulled me out of my daze.

Grabbing the mouse, I opened the notification. My heart slammed against my ribcage as I scanned the map on the screen, unsure if I believed what I was seeing. "Caroline activated her tracker. She's still in Alabama."

Scarlett gasped, her hand flying to her mouth. "Oh, my gosh. Do you think... Is she..."

Hope and fear warred within me, and I was too scared to allow one to win the fight. "I don't know yet, but we've got a lead. Finally, a real lead."

My fingers flew across the keyboard, homing in on the signal, calculating the location. Once I had it, I grabbed my phone, my fingers fumbling to dial Ethan's number. He answered on the first ring.

"Tristan? What's up?" There was the distinct sound of scraping in the background, making me wonder what I had interrupted, but I didn't question it. I was not sure I wanted to know.

"It's Caroline," I said, the adrenaline pumping through my system making it difficult to sit still. "She activated the tracker I gave her. She's still in Alabama, a few hours from here."

There was a grunt, then a loud thump in the background, and I did not need Ethan to tell me he'd been in the middle of an interrogation, and that whoever was in the room with him was no longer breathing. "Where? Can you pinpoint it?"

Zooming in on the screen, I scanned the maps and data. "I'm trying. The signal is coming from a heavily-wooded area northwest of here—near the state line. But it's deep in the southern Appalachians, so from the map I can't even make out any buildings or dwellings of any kind."

"Text me the exact coordinates the second you have them," he said, and then I heard him already moving, keys jangling. "I'm leaving New Orleans now. I'll get there as fast as I can."

When the call went dead, I turned to Scarlett, and there was an unspoken understanding between us before she nodded, pulling Evie closer to her. "Go," she said, stepping away from the doorway. "Evie and I will be safe here. Bring our girl home."

I was not an assassin like Ethan, or a violent person, but I knew how to shoot a gun, and I couldn't sit around and wait five hours for Ethan to get back. Not when I knew where Caroline was.

Pulling Evie and then Scarlett into a hug, I did my best to settle the fire burning inside me just enough to process my thoughts. "I'm going to find her. I promise."

Scarlett pulled away, her dark eyes glazed with unshed tears. "Be careful, Tristan. Don't take any unnecessary risks. Scope the place out but wait for him to move. *Please.*"

Reaching for my bag, I shoved my laptop and a few other pieces of tech inside, not knowing what I would need. "I'll be okay. I need to do this." I glanced over at Evie, who was watching our exchange silently. "For her."

Scarlett followed my gaze and nodded. "Hurry back. All of you."

With one final look at Scarlett and Evie, I threw my backpack over my shoulder and headed out of the safe room, staying only long enough to hear the locks click into place.

When I was sure they would be safe, I headed into the room where Ethan kept his weapons. I grabbed a 9mm from the locker, checking the clip and sliding it into its holster before connecting it to my belt. I had spent enough time in a gun range blowing off steam to know how to use it, although I hoped I wouldn't have to. With the gun secured, I armed myself with backup ammunition and a few more weapons, including two knives, and headed back up the stairs.

Doubt flitted through my mind as I checked the exterior cameras and motion sensors from my device, making sure no one was on the property before slipping out of the cabin and heading toward the barn where I had parked. Ethan expected me to stay at the cabin with Scarlett and Evie until he returned, but I did not stop walking. I knew he would probably be pissed that I'd left, and maybe I was doing the wrong thing, but I knew the cabin's security measures would keep Scarlett and Evie safe. They would be fine without me there, but Caroline's safety was not known. She needed me more, so even with Ethan's instructions lingering in the back of my mind, I turned the key in the ignition and headed northwest.

CHAPTER 26

The Savior

The dingy walls of the safe house pressed in around me as I sat in front of the computer. I had already been there for a day, and aside from research, I felt no closer to finding my sister. Ivy's files taunted me, a jumble of information on a thumb drive he had given me the last time I saw him that I knew could be entirely useless.

Sighing, I ran my hand through my hair, clicking through what was stored on the device. Everything around me reminded me of the man I was before I had met Scarlett—the ruthless assassin who ended lives without a second thought. Now here I was, trying to save a life...again.

My sister's name echoed in my mind as I scanned the files, looking specifically for any mention of Delacroix's known associates, headquarters, or hangouts. I could not listen from the shadows if I didn't know where the remaining members of Delacroix's gang were lingering.

So much guilt twisted in my gut as I thought about all the potential places and states of being my sister could be in. These men were monsters, and she was out there somewhere, in danger because of me, because I could not protect her. The one thing I did not think her captors had considered was that she had a bigger monster on her team, and her monster wasn't fighting because of a payout... Her monster would destroy them because of love.

As I scrolled through the files and emails on Ivy's thumb drive, I came across a bar near the port owned by a close friend of Delacroix, Marcel. According to Ivy's notes, it was frequented by Delacroix's men. It was a long shot, especially with the FBI sniffing around, but any lead was better than nothing.

Grabbing my keys and holstering my weapons, I rushed out into the muggy night air.

The streets of New Orleans were busy at such a late hour, but the closer I got to the port, the more the crowd thinned. The air was heavy, more so than just from the humidity. There was always a dark, macabre weight to New Orleans that crawled across your skin and sat on your shoulders to witness any despicable things you did under its influence. Some would say it was the spirits who gave it the reputation of being one of the most haunted cities in the country. But I did not believe in such things. Perhaps if I did, I would not have made a career out of leaving so many more ghosts in my wake.

Parking my car in an alley two blocks away, I pulled my hood over my head and slid my gun into my pocket. From where I was parked, I could see Marcel's bar, a rundown building with neon signs flickering in the windows. There were a few motorcycles parked out front, as well as a few vehicles in the alley behind the building. People who were perhaps trying to stay off the radar...just like me.

Sixties and seventies rock blared from the jukebox inside the bar, the air filled with smoke and the smell of stale liquor. A few patrons lingered at the dimly lit bar while another handful sat at tables around the space. I felt their weathered faces watching me, but I did not meet anyone's stare. The less people who saw my face the better.

Approaching the bar on the more shadowed side, I slid onto the bar stool, lifting my hand to order a whiskey, never looking the bartender in the face as he dropped off my drink and took my money. Instead, I scanned the room, listening in as snatches of conversations drifted to me, mentions of jobs, money, and trouble.

I sat there for a while, sipping slowly on the whiskey in my hand, not wanting it to dull my senses. There was a high chance that I was going to need my strength and my wits before the end of the night. A few more guys walked into the bar as I sat there, taking a seat at a table in the corner where a lone patron had been all night. Mere moments passed before a conversation started up that I was more than a little interested in.

"Heard there's a bounty on that Prejean broad and her old man, Etienne. Fifty grand for the bitch, hundred for her father."

My fingers tightened around the gun in my pocket, rage boiling in my veins at hearing them speak about my wife in that way. If I had time later, I intended to remove their tongues for daring to disrespect her.

I signaled the bartender for another drink, even though the one in my hand was still mostly full, using the motion to glance at the men in the corner. Although I could not tell if they were Delacroix's thugs or just a couple of Cajun shit-talkers, it was clear in their body language that they believed everything they said, which made me think there must have been at least a flicker of truth to their claims.

"And that Italian who took over for Delacroix wants them alive, at least for now."

Tossing a bill onto the bar, I stood, watching as one of the men at the corner table walked toward the back of the bar, heading toward the bathroom. "You have a good night now," I said as I walked away, however I did not leave.

With my hand on the blade in my pocket, I followed the taller mobster into the hallway, but before he could push open the bathroom door, I shoved him through the back door instead and into a darkened alley. He startled, spinning around, but I already had him pinned to the exterior wall, forearm crushing his throat.

"Where is she?" I growled.

Panic flooded his eyes as he struggled for air, so I eased up just enough for him to rasp, "Who?"

Not in the mood for his stupidity, I slammed him against the wall again. "Don't play dumb with me. Where the hell is the girl they took for Aresco?"

He sputtered something unintelligible, clawing at my arm. Snatching the knife from my pocket, I pressed it under his chin, cold metal biting into his skin.

"Last chance," I warned, enunciating every word. "Where. Is. She?"

"I don't know!" he choked out, his brown eyes wild with fear. "Aresco put out a bounty on her, and I heard some guys were hunting her, but I don't know where they took her!"

Hunting. The word was like a knife to my gut, twisting deep. I should have done more to protect her.

Having already scoped out the area, and needing to get him somewhere with more privacy, I dragged him away from the back of the bar. Fury burned through my veins, barely contained beneath my skin. He stumbled and fell to his knees, gasping for air and only pissing me off more.

"Please," he rasped, hands held up in surrender. "I told you the truth."

"You're only still alive because you may still be useful." Grabbing him by the collar, I hauled him to his feet and shoved him toward the abandoned building down the alley. "So, you'd better think really hard about how badly you want to keep those secrets."

The old storage building was decrepit, needing nothing more than to be torched, but it was the closest place I knew I would be able to interrogate him further without his screams being heard by passersby.

With my knife put away and my gun in my hand so he would not fight, I bound his hands and ankles to a chair, the light of the moon providing the only illumination.

Once he was tied up securely, I opened up my duffle bag and pulled out my blade and my catfish skinning pliers. Somewhere, Aresco had Caroline, and this pathetic waste of flesh was going to tell me exactly where she was.

For twenty minutes, I pulled the skin from three of his fingers, gagging him to keep him from making too much noise. Still, he kept repeating the same stories, and my patience was running thin. Rage burning through me, I pressed the blade to his throat again. He was wasting my time. "Last chance. Where is she?"

He whimpered through the cloth, moisture puddling on the ground beneath him. "I told you. I don't know!"

All I wanted was to slit his lying throat, but then he would not be able to give up his men. I slammed my fist into his jaw instead, relishing the crack of bone.

"Useless piece of shit," I spat, stalking away. My hands shook with the urge to hurt him, to make him talk, but it was no use. Either he did not know anything, or he didn't have enough of a sense of self preservation to choose himself over them. Either way, he was a dead man.

As I paced, he slumped against his bindings, whimpering through bloodied lips. Just as I was debating slicing his throat and being done with him, a sharp ring shattered through my thoughts, sending my pulse racing. I answered it on the first ring, dragging my blade against the table to remove some of the flesh.

"Tristan. What's up?"

"It's Caroline," he said, panic clear in his tone. "She activated the tracker I gave her. She's still in Alabama, a few hours from here."

Heart flipping in my chest, I closed the distance between myself and the groaning man on the chair, slicing his throat, the dropping weight of his body making the chair fall over. I barely paid him any mind. He was useless to me. "Where? Can you pinpoint it?"

Tristan went silent for a minute, giving me time to spread the gasoline I had left in the alley all over the interior of the structure. "I'm trying. The signal is coming from a heavily-wooded area northwest of here—near the state line. But it's deep in the southern Appalachians, so from the map I can't even make out any buildings or dwellings of any kind."

"Text me the exact coordinates the second you have them," I said, tossing a match on the dead man's body before stepping out of the building. "I'm leaving New Orleans now. I'll get there as fast as I can."

CHAPTER 27

The Phoenix

I awoke with a start, my eyes blinking open to nothing but inky blackness. The lumpy mattress pressed into my back as a dull throb pulsed through my body. After finding the tracking device on my watch, I pressed the activation button, hoping the signal would find its way to Tristan. At some point after that, my body had given up, and I had passed out. I was not sure how long I'd been sleeping, but it was nighttime outside. It could have been a day or three later... I was not sure.

Willing the nausea twisting in my gut to subside, I took a steadying breath, blowing out slowly. I could not afford to lose the little food I'd been given, especially after vomiting when I'd overheard them discussing selling me on the black market. Just thinking about it made acid rise in my throat, but I pushed it down. Weakness was a luxury I could not afford if I wanted to survive this, and at least for the moment, I wanted to survive.

For Evie, I told myself. I had to stay strong for my daughter. She was out there somewhere, waiting for me to come home. After already losing her daddy, I could not take her mommy too.

Gritting my teeth against the pain, I shifted onto my side, fear making it hard to breathe. The thin mattress did little to cushion my body as I shifted, trying to sit up. The movement sent pain radiating through my ribs and I had to bite my lip to keep from crying out. As gently as I could, I reached down to feel along my side. Definitely bruised, if not fractured. I took as deep of a breath as I could manage, but it felt as if there was a knife in my side. Definitely fractured.

Fear threatened to overwhelm me, but I pushed it down. I knew I had to keep a level head if I was going to get out of my predicament, but the walls closed in around me as I sat in the dark, my mind racing as it tried to formulate a plan, but nothing came. I was too weak. Too tired. Too beaten down.

A tear slid down my cheek as Evie's face floated before my eyes and I swiped it roughly, as angry at my emotions as I was at the world. It had proven to be a cruel place, but I was not ready to give up the fight. The glass shard I had clutched in my hand before finding the tracking device confirmed it. My hesitation seemed almost foolish when the footsteps came, but the glass shard...

Heart hammering against my tender ribs, I slid off the mattress and slipped my hand beneath it where I had hidden the makeshift blade, blowing out a breath when my fingers touched its jagged edge. I knew it would not save me in a fight against multiple armed men, but something inside me felt safer knowing it was there.

The sound of heavy footsteps echoed down the hallway outside, my breath catching in my throat as they drew nearer. I steeled myself, begging my nerves to settle, because the more fear I showed, the more it seemed to egg them on.

The lock on the door clicked loudly in the silence, the hinges creaking as the heavy door swung inward. Harsh light flooded the small room, blinding me momentarily. Squinting against the glare, numbness flooded through my limbs when I recognized the familiar silhouette in the doorway, flanked by his two henchmen.

With a confident stride, the long-haired man stepped through the threshold, rolling up the sleeves of his button-down black shirt. His presence was overwhelming in the confined space, and for a moment, I regretted the hesitation that had convinced me to slide the glass beneath the mattress rather than across my wrist. Whether I spoke to him or did not, it always seemed to cause the same outcome, and I didn't know what to do anymore. Aside from hoping Ethan and Tristan would find me, there did not seem to be any other way out.

"Ready to talk now? Or do you need more convincing?"

Scooting back until my back hit the wall, I said nothing, clenching my jaw. He closed the distance between us in an instant, grabbing my chin and jerking my face up to his. The stale smoke on his breath nearly made me gag. "Whether you tell us where to find Ivy Etienne or not, we will eventually find your father. The only difference is whether you want to live longer than him."

His words hung heavy in the air, a challenge laid bare. I bit the inside of my cheek until I tasted blood. There was no way I could tell him where Scarlett was, and I did not know where her father was. I was fighting a losing battle, no matter which way I looked at it. The weight of his demands was suffocating, and I already could barely breathe.

Wrenching my head from his grip, I glared at him defiantly. There was no warmth in his gaze, only the icy indifference of a man who had long ago surrendered any semblance of empathy. Under his intimidating shadow, I struggled to maintain my composure, to project an image of indifference despite the tremors that betrayed me. I wondered how close I could get to the glass shard beneath the mattress—how quickly I could slit his throat before one of his buddies put a bullet in me.

His eyes darkened at my refusal to speak, annoyance making his nostrils flare. In a flash, his hand shot out, grabbing me by the throat and slamming me against the wall. Struggling against his hold, I gasped for air, my ribs screaming.

"Let's try this again," he hissed through gritted teeth. "Because I'm really trying to be patient. Where has the old man gone?"

I clawed at his hand, struggling to breathe. Black spots swam before my eyes, my head spinning. Just when I thought I might pass out, he released me and took a step back. I doubled over, coughing and wheezing. He did not go far. Instead, he crouched down, forcing me to meet his relentless gaze. "You have one last chance. Tell me where he is, or I'll send my men back to find the daughter you're trying to get back to."

A jolt of fear pierced my heart at the mention of her, making me regret ever mentioning I had a child. An idea formed in my mind—a desperate gamble to stall—but my only play.

Slumping against the wall and sliding down onto the mattress, I let my eyes roll back, going limp as I feigned unconsciousness. A tense beat of silence followed, but the slide of shoes against the concrete told me he had stepped back.

"Fuck," he spat. "Check her."

Rough hands grabbed at me, probing for a pulse, but I kept my body limp. After a moment, the man touching me moved away. "She's still breathing, but it's shallow," he said, a note of concern threading through the words. Not necessarily in concern for me, however. It was clear I was worth money to them—probably more alive than dead. "What if she doesn't—"

"Then, we have a problem," the long-haired man interrupted, the vitriol in his voice unmistakable.

Every fiber of my being screamed to fight, to rise and face them with the ferocity of a mother whose child was in danger, but my body betrayed me, refusing to heed the call to arms. Instead, I remained limp on the lumpy mattress that might as well have been my pyre.

Holding my breath, I prayed my ruse would work. The long-haired man cursed again, but he did not move closer.

Finally, he sighed and took a few more steps away from me. "Leave her. We'll deal with her later. For now, let's see how long she lasts."

The door clicked shut with the finality of a tomb sealing closed, and then their footsteps receded, leaving me alone with the oppressive darkness that seemed to press down upon me with the weight of my fear.

Slowly, cautiously, I opened my eyes. The room around me swam into focus. I may have faked passing out, but I was not completely pretending. Each breath was a battle, the air thick and stale against my lips. I forced myself to inhale deeply, to find the steel that had seen me through the lonely nights and the endless hospital stays with Evie, but dread pooled in my stomach, a leaden weight that threatened to drag me under. At least for a little while, I let it take me.

CHAPTER 28

The Phantom

The air was heavy with the scent of pine and damp earth as I parked my car at the foot of a trail that snaked its way into the heart of the Appalachian wilderness. I had been driving for two hours with the music loud enough to drown out my racing thoughts, but the minute I climbed out of the car, the weight of the night pressed against me, a thick blanket of darkness that seemed to absorb all sound and movement. It was too quiet.

Reaching into the backseat, I retrieved my backpack, which held the extra weapons and ammo, binoculars, water, laptop, compass, among a few other things. My stomach twisted as I climbed back into my car and pulled out my phone, needing to make a call I did not want to make where my voice wouldn't carry. There was a chance Ethan would be pissed that I went against his direction and left Scarlett and Evie alone at the cabin, but I could not find it in myself to regret my decision.

Fingers trembling slightly, I dialed Ethan's number. He answered on the first ring, his voice tight with tension. "I'm still two hours out. Any updates? Scarlett and Evie—"

"I'm here at the location," I interrupted, needing to get the words out. "Scarlett and Evie are still in the safe room. They're fine."

There was a pause, and I could almost hear Ethan's mind racing, weighing the risks. Or maybe he was planning how to kill me when he saw me. "Damnit, Tristan," he finally replied, his tone laced with both frustration and under-standing. "You should have waited for backup. If anything happens to them..."

A knot tightened in my stomach, but I shook my head. "Nothing will happen to them. They're secure. But Caro-line... We can't afford to lose more time."

Ethan let out a heavy sigh, the sound like static in my ear. "Alright. Stake out the place but keep your head down. I'm on my way. Don't do anything until I get there."

"Understood. Be careful," I said, the words seeming inad-equate, but I did not know what else to say.

"Always am," was all he said and then the line went dead.

Climbing out of the car, I tucked my phone away, allowing myself a moment to breathe in the night air, trying to calm my nerves, but it was useless. I was out of my element, so I was running on pure adrenaline and the need to rescue the woman I cared deeply for. I just hoped I had not made an unwise decision that would get us both killed.

The darkness of the Appalachian Forest swallowed me whole, a silent behemoth that stood indifferent to the urgency pulsing through my veins. Every step I took was a careful negotiation with the terrain, the coordinates of Caroline's tracker leading me deeper into the heart of the timbered maze. The beam from my flashlight cut through the night, illuminating tangled underbrush and gnarled roots ready to trip an unwary traveler. I just did not want it to be me.

The ground beneath my feet was damp, my boots sinking into the moss and fallen leaves making subtle noises that disrupted the silence I was trying to maintain. Yet, there was still a stillness that hung in the air the deeper I went, punctuated only by the distant hoot of an owl or the rustle of nocturnal creatures stirring in the undergrowth. It was as if nature herself was holding her breath, waiting for the outcome of my quest.

Navigating through this verdant labyrinth, I remained vigilant, my senses attuned to any anomaly, any sign that would indicate danger lurking just beyond the reach of my light. The digital world had always been where I felt most at ease, a realm of clarity and control so starkly contrasted by the unpredictable chaos of the forest. Yet there I was, driven by a force stronger than any code or algorithm—my burgeoning connection to Caroline—what I was starting to suspect could be love.

An hour passed—a lifetime in each minute—as I followed the old logging road, now little more than a whisper of its former self. The ghost of industry wound through the forest, a reminder of man's fleeting dominion over nature. And then, like a specter emerging from the past, a warehouse appeared, dilapidated and all but consumed by the encroaching wilderness—but not uninhabited.

With the stealth of the Phantom I was, I found refuge behind a grouping of trees, their branches providing a canopy of concealment. From the vantage point, I made out the silhouette of a building, its structure imposing and out of place in the otherwise untamed landscape. The moon, a sliver of silver in the sky, illuminated the broken windows high on the exterior, too small and high for anyone to climb out—at least from what I could tell. Still, I wondered if I would be able to find a way to get up high enough to peek inside, possibly find where they were keeping her.

Heart a steady drumbeat in my chest, I settled into my hidden perch, muscles taught. Each moment that ticked by was a moment too long, a stretch of time in which Caroline's fate hung in the balance. Watching from outside, I could not help but imagine what she could be suffering through just inside, and it made me want to go in after her, but I knew I needed to wait for Ethan. If we were going to be successful, we needed to work together.

Knowing I had nothing but time until Ethan got there, I lifted the binoculars to my eyes, narrowing my focus on the decrepit structure that held Caroline captive. The night vision lenses brought the scene into sharp detail—the grainy textures of the weathered walls, the jagged shards of glass clinging to the window frames like desperate fingers, and the slow prowl of shadows cast by the moon's gaze.

One by one, I counted the mobsters lingering outside—eight in total—their outlines ghosting through my field of vision. They moved like they had no care in the world, guns slung casually over shoulders, cigarettes dangling from lips, their laughter grinding over my already taut nerves. Watching them closely, I memorized their positions. There were two by the entrance, lethargic and unsuspecting, one of them actually sleeping as he leaned against the wall. Several feet away, there were three men clustered near a flickering fire barrel, the shadows dancing across their hard, lined faces telling me they were at least in their forties. Another trio patrolled in a loose arc, using flashlights to check the tree line for any trespassers.

From what I could tell, the building didn't appear to have power, but was instead being lit by candles and a generator that was loud when it kicked on, but it seemed as though they didn't run the generator during the entire night, unless they needed it to power something for a short period of time. It had kicked on once since I had been watching them, but it only ran for about twenty minutes before turning off. If the generator was powered on when Ethan and I went in to try to rescue Caroline, I knew it would provide us with reliable sound cover. If I could find a way to turn it on without them knowing it was not one of them who did it, then we could use it as a distraction.

A rustle of leaves, so slight it could have been mistaken for wind, snatched my attention. A long figure skirted the edge of the clearing, his silhouette fragmenting as he passed between trees and moonlight. With his path meandering too close to where I crouched, I had to make a decision—one I wouldn't be able to come back from.

Sliding the hunting knife out of its sheath, I burrowed farther back into the brush, allowing the night to cloak me. I peered around the tree's bulk, watching the mobster pause, head cocked as if sensing me, but he seemed to shake his unease off and continued to walk in my direction. Without a sound, I stood, back pressed against the dark side of the tree, listening as his footsteps got closer and closer, my heart beating in time with his steps.

When he stopped right next to my hiding spot, I held my breath, planning my attack, but before I could strike him, another pair of eyes slipped out of the forest behind him. Before I could even register what was happening, Ethan grabbed the mobster by the back of his jacket and pulled the man closer, dragging an insanely long blade across the guard's neck. I stood there motionless as I watched the mobster's body slump to the ground, blood spilling out in rivers onto the forest floor, doing my best to keep the contents of my stomach intact. I had never witnessed such violence in person before. It wasn't something I thought would be easy to wipe from my mind, but although I was not a violent person, and wasn't looking forward to taking *any* life, I knew it had to be done, and I knew we would both do whatever we had to do in order to save Caroline. If that meant I would have to kill to do it, then so be it.

"Hey," he whispered, wiping his blade on the jacket of the dead guy at our feet. "Were you going to kill him? Or buy him a drink?"

I huffed, the tension that had wound itself around my spine unraveling as I lowered my weapon. "Thought you would never show. Scarlett and Evie?"

Reaching forward, Ethan grabbed my binoculars and held them up to his eyes. "I spoke to her right before getting here. They're in the safe room and locked down tight."

"Good." I nodded, a little bit of reassurance settling over me like a cloak. With them safe, we could focus on keeping Caroline—and ourselves—safe.

"Any sign of Caroline?" Ethan's voice broke through the haze of my thoughts, dragging my attention back to the task at hand.

"Nothing yet," I admitted, the worry for her gnawing at me like a persistent ache.

When he turned his eyes to me, there was a hint of mischief in them, as though he enjoyed the rush. "Then, let's get her back."

CHAPTER 29

The Savior

Tristan crouched beside me, his eyes scanning the grim facade of the warehouse as if he could pierce its secrets with sheer will. Caroline was in there, a prisoner. Rage simmered in my veins, but I tamped it down. It may have been months since I had worn my darkness on the outside, but it had slipped on like my favorite pair of boots.

"We've got six guards on rotation," he murmured, my own gaze tracking the sweep of a flashlight's beam through the tangled brush. "Two by the main entrance, two roaming, and the two who are supposed to be at the back are by the fire barrel. There were two others, but one went inside and the other is dead on the ground. So, aside from whoever is inside, there are six left."

The corner of my lips lifted into a grin, even though my hands curled into fists, leather cracking. "You went through that like a pro. Consistency is good, though. Makes 'em predictable." Shifting my weight, I jerked my chin at the building. "Cameras?"

Tristan shook his head, the ghost of a smile touching his lips as though proud of himself. "They're using a generator, so they have cheap cameras—portable ones run by batteries. I was able to tap into them and disable them with my cellphone."

"Alright, then." I ran a hand through my hair before pulling my hoodie over my head. Tristan did the same. If we were going to find my sister, we needed to blend into the shadows. "We'll pick off the guards on patrol first, since it'll be easier to hide from their buddies. Then, we will hit the two guys in the back," I said, straightening my legs. "We're getting her out of there—tonight."

The pale moon cast its silvery glow over the forest, but the brush was thick, allowing us to move like ghosts through the darkness. I had given Tristan specific instructions on his part in the rescue because I knew he was out of his element, no matter how badly he wanted to find her. Still, he was armed, and he was a big guy, so if he had the opportunity to take a guard down, then I wanted him to do it. I just did not want to see something happen to him, or to have him taken too, not when I already had Caroline to save.

Moving through the trees toward the warehouse, my blade was a comforting weight in my hand, the hilt worn smooth from years of use. Two shadows detached from the tree line ahead, lumbering into view—the guards making their rounds.

Before they could see us, I reached for Tristan's arm, pulling him deeper into the foliage, where we waited for them to pass our position. Tristan slid a hunting knife out of the holster at his thigh, making me just a little bit proud.

As the two mobsters sauntered past, seeming to not have a care in the world, I stepped out onto the trail behind them. My arm snaked around the nearest guard's throat, cutting off his airway before he could make a sound. When his buddy turned to see what was going on, Tristan struck out with his knife, catching the other guy in the stomach. He crumpled to his knees with a choked cry, arms wrapped around his middle.

The guard in my grasp scratched uselessly at my arm, his gun dangling from his shoulder. "Shh," I whispered, tightening my hold. "It will all be over soon."

His struggles ceased within moments as my blade severed his spinal cord. Stepping around to where his buddy was still on the ground, barely conscious as he bled out, I had no problems putting him out of his misery.

Leaving the two gangsters where they fell, we pressed on, and I wondered if the darkness within me would ever truly fade away, or if I was forever doomed to carry the burden. One thing was for certain, I would do whatever it took to protect the ones I loved, even if it meant sacrificing a piece of myself in the process, but with Scarlett and our daughter on the way, I needed to be a better man. I needed to be worthy of them—something I knew I would never be—but my Little Red disagreed, and fuck if I did not love her for it.

In the cover of the forest, we made our way around the ramshackle building that looked so out of place in the dense forest. I was not sure what it was previously used for, but judging from the exterior, I thought it may have been used for logging, but it had clearly been vacant for decades, judging not only from the condition of the structure but from the logging road as well. From what I could see, the kidnappers had probably been forced to hike in as well, as there were no vehicles parked nearby.

Pausing near the side of the building, I peered around the corner toward the back entrance, spotting the two guards who still lingered near a fire barrel. The cherry of a cigarette illuminated the face of one, but the other had his back to me, both men seeming completely clueless as to our presence as they chatted on. Flicking his cigarette, the one facing our direction muttered something to his friend and walked toward the other side of the building, probably to take a piss.

I met Tristan's gaze, holding up two fingers. His jaw tightened, but he gave a curt nod, knowing what needed to be done, even if he did not like it.

"One of them just went around the building to take a piss," I whispered, gripping the hilt of my weapon. "Stay here. If I don't return, make sure you get inside that door."

There was a brief flash of panic across Tristan's eyes, but he masked it quickly and nodded, his hand tightening on the knife at his side.

Leaving Tristan where he stood, I crept around to the other side of the building, peeking around the corner. It took a moment for me to find him with how dark it was, but luckily my target was a chain smoker, so the flame of his lighter caught my attention as he stepped into the trees. I took a quick scan of the area around me and then stepped in behind him. Before he had a chance to pull out his cock, I reached for him, pressing my blade against his throat, and tugging him against my front.

"Scream and my hand slips," I said, putting a tiny bit more pressure against his skin.

He stilled, his cigarette hitting the ground at our feet. "Whaddya want man?"

My hand tightened around his other arm, making damn sure he did not touch his weapon. "The girl. Where is she?"

"Wh-what girl, man? I dunno what you're talkin' about."

"Wrong answer, buddy." Tsking, I pressed my knife a little deeper, until I knew it broke his skin. A pathetic whine left his lips, but he did not fight. "If you want your head still attached to your body when your family sees you again, you'll tell me where the girl is."

His body tensed, but he did not budge. "She's in one of the storage rooms near the front offices, b-but she's in bad shape, man. Aresco's man did a number on her."

A toxic mix of rage and dread fueled my movements as I sliced into his throat, my ears ringing as I walked away from him and back toward Tristan. I did not stop when I found him where I'd left him and instead continued forward, toward the unsuspecting guard with his back toward me. There was no hesitation when I plunged my knife into his back, and I did not care if he was still breathing when I reached for the door. My sister was hurt, and there was nothing that would stand in my way of getting to her.

Tristan caught up with me as I turned the handle and peeked in through the door, but he remained silent. Although we had taken out five of the guards outside, we had no way to know how many people were inside. It was on the list of questions I had planned to ask, but hearing my sister was in bad shape had changed my priorities.

The shadows embraced us as we slipped inside the decrepit warehouse, the tang of rust and damp wood saturating the stale air. The darkness was almost suffocating, but it was our only protection. The blood of the two back door guards still dripped off my blade as I stared into the darkness, but I did not care. There would be more soon. My heart hammered in my chest, threatening to burst, but I did my best to remain calm. Somewhere in the labyrinth of abandoned offices and equipment, my sister was being held captive. I could not let the panic take hold, though it gnawed at my edges like a rabid dog.

Leaving the door to freedom behind, we moved through the cavernous warehouse, barely more than shadows ourselves as we wove between hulking machines shrouded in tarps. Each sound seemed amplified, the drop of water from a leaky pipe, our own breaths growing ragged with tension. The only thing I did not hear were voices. I had no idea where the others were, but I knew they were there. With it being almost sunrise, I hoped they were asleep. Without electricity, it was nearly impossible to see, so we followed the corridor toward the direction of the front of the building, hoping it was the right way.

The faint whiff of cigarette smoke met my nose as we turned the corner to find two guards lingering in the hallway before us. There was no way to hide from their view, and my instincts told me the door behind them would lead me to Caroline, so I lunged.

The first guard charged toward me, swinging a baton at my head. Ducking out of the way, I drove my blade into his gut, and he crumpled to the floor with a groan.

Jumping over him, the second guard pulled a knife from his belt and lunged at us. I sidestepped the attack and delivered a sharp blow to the back of his head. He staggered back, temporarily dazed, but stayed on his feet.

Not giving him time to recover, I moved in, slashing at him with my blade. He was clearly an experienced fighter and parried my strikes. Before I could move out of the way, he kicked me hard in the chest. The wind knocked out of me, I stumbled back. The guard pressed his advantage, raining down blows with his knife. I blocked what I could, but the knife found my shoulder, slicing through my hoodie and meeting skin. Against the wall, the other guard returned to his feet, fumbling for the gun in his holster. Running out from behind me, Tristan reached for his arm, fighting to wrench the gun free.

Seeing me temporarily distracted, my opponent rushed for me, the bloody knife in his hand. Gritting my teeth against the pain in my shoulder, my blade hit the ground as I grabbed his wrist.

For several long moments, we struggled over the knife, my energy waning. At the last second, as my arm threatened to give out, Tristan grabbed the guard from behind and pulled him into a chokehold. Turning away from me altogether, the guard struggled violently, but Tristan's grip was like iron. With a final spasm, the guard went limp in Tristan's arms and then dropped to the ground. I wasted no time bending over to pick up my blade and send him to the same place as his friends.

With the guards bleeding out on the concrete and my shoulder wrapped in a strip of my torn shirt, Tristan and I stood before the metal door, the only barrier between us and Caroline. My hand trembled as I slid the key I had taken from one of the guards into the lock, fear from what I would find on the other side nearly paralyzing.

The door screeched on rusted hinges as dim light from the hallway spilled into the darkened room. My heart lurched when I saw the outline of a figure crumpled on the floor.

"Caroline," I rasped, rushing to her side with Tristan on my heels. She lay frighteningly still, her eyes closed. Bruises mottled her pale skin. Dried blood stained her lips.

Tristan reached for her, but before he could touch her, I scooped her up, cradling her head against my chest. "Caroline, can you hear me?"

Eyes fluttering open halfway, she tried to speak but only managed a broken whimper.

Raged welled inside me, white-hot. I tried to stand, but pain shot through my shoulder, nearly making me drop her.

"Take her," I told Tristan, panic filling me as I held her out in front of me. "We have to get her out of here."

With Caroline secured in Tristan's arms, I pulled out one of my pistols, anticipating further confrontation. We stepped back out into the dark corridor, my senses on high alert. At every turn, I expected more guards to appear. Caroline's breathing was labored in Tristan's arms behind me, each whimper a stab to my heart. I should have found her sooner.

Rounding the corner, we came face to face with two more mobsters blocking our path. Tristan cursed under his breath and laid Caroline down inside an open doorway to keep her out of harm's way.

As the taller one with long hair lunged and knocked my gun out of my hand, I pivoted, ramming my elbow up under his jaw. He reeled back with a garbled shout. In a flash, my knife was in my hand. I slashed at him, driving him back. Dimly, I was aware of his companion grappling with Tristan behind me, but before I could turn to make sure Caroline was okay, the long-haired man barreled into me, slamming me against the wall. My knife skittered away across the floor. Time slowed as we grappled with each other, exchanging blows. I was injured, but I was fueled by rage and desperation, so the pain did not phase me.

With a burst of energy, I twisted free and smashed my fist into his throat. He choked, clawing at his neck. Before he could regain his composure, I followed up with a kick to his gut, then a swing to his head. He collapsed in a heap.

Panting, I scooped up my gun and turned to where Tristan was still wrestling against the other mobster. Without taking a breath, I fired. I had had enough.

Blood and brain matter sprayed across the wall as the mobster hit the ground in front of me. Tristan did not hesitate to scoop Caroline up off the ground, holding her close.

"Get her to your car and to safety," I said, no room for argument in my command.

Tristan's gaze dropped to my blood-soaked shirt. "You're hurt. You might—"

"I'll live. Go."

Only hesitating for a moment longer, he slipped past me and into the night, Caroline's dark hair spilling over his arm. The moment the door shut behind him, I bolted for the machine room we had walked through when first arriving. Metal barrels were stacked high in the corner, the sharp tang of gasoline meeting my nose. Moving as quickly as I could, I kicked them over and opened the valves, leaving a trailing line of fuel as I walked toward the exit.

There, I opened the door and paused, steeling myself. Then I lit a match and dropped it to the gasoline-soaked floor.

Flames erupted with a roar, racing hungrily along the fuel line, devouring everything in their path. I slipped outside, the blistering heat at my back as I fled into the forest.

CHAPTER 30
The Phoenix

A faint light blinded me as my eyes fluttered open, the searing pain throbbing in my temple pulsing with each heartbeat. I blinked rapidly, trying to clear the fog from my vision. The ground beneath me vibrated, but I did not know if I was actually moving, or if it was all in my head. Panic swelled in my chest, and I jolted up, struggling to see out of my swollen eye. "Evie!"

"Caroline," a soft, familiar voice said, a hand reaching over to grab mine. I flinched away, waiting for the strike. "Caroline, it's me."

The car slowed and I leaned back on the seat, turning to look at the driver as we came to a stop. "It's me, Superwoman. You're safe now."

Although I knew it was probably a dream, or perhaps something more final, I gazed into the face of Tristan, his hazel green eyes etched with concern behind dark frame glasses. "Tristan?"

Hand hovering in the air between us for a moment, he placed it on mine, squeezing gently. "You're safe now, Caroline. I promise, I won't let anyone hurt you again."

I could not find it in myself to believe it was real, but overwhelming relief flooded through my body anyway, sending tears from my eyes that I never gave permission to fall. "Evie?"

Hesitating for a moment, he leaned forward, pulling me against his chest. Everything hurt, my body battered and bruised, but I allowed him to hold me in his arms as I sobbed. "Evie's safe, love. She's safe at home with Scarlett. Ethan is on his way home behind us. Everyone is safe."

Even though my mind still believed none of it was true, I nodded against his chest, giving the words permission to sink in. "Take me to see her. *Please*."

After a moment longer, he pressed a kiss to my cheek, and then shifted the car back into drive, but he did not let go of my hand. I was grateful for it, because it was the only thing keeping me grounded in the moment as I sank back into the leather seat.

The incessant throbbing in my head was the first thing I noticed as I slowly regained consciousness. My body ached all over, but my head and my ribs were the worst.

"We're almost there," Tristan said, his voice low and soothing. Still holding my hand, his thumb rubbed my knuckles, sending a shiver through me even as the rest of me was in agony.

Through the car window, I watched the trees rushing past. It was a road I recognized. We were nearing the cabin, nearing safety.

Arriving outside Ethan and Scarlett's cabin, the car rolled to a stop and Tristan killed the engine. My door opened a moment later, the early morning air raising goosebumps on my skin, and then Tristan's arm slipped beneath me. When he lifted me out of the car, I allowed my battered frame to lean against him, drawing upon his strength as though it was the very air I breathed. The emotion that poured out of me as we ascended the steps, and he opened the door was unrestrained. Raw and freeing.

The familiar scent of pine enveloped me as he stepped over the threshold and closed the door behind us, but the house was quiet. Although the sunrise would bring with it a certain level of safety that could not be guaranteed in the night, Scarlett and Evie were undoubtedly still in the safe room downstairs. I was relieved by that.

"I don't want her to see me like this," I said, not looking up to meet his face. For the past few days, I'd wanted nothing more in the world than to be with my daughter, but I realized that I wasn't ready. I didn't want to scare her with how horrible I knew I looked. "Not yet."

Tristan nodded, heading down the hall toward the guest room. My legs trembled as he set me down, barely able to carry my weight, but I remained standing on my own two feet. The chill of the porcelain sink pressed against my palms as I leaned heavily, catching my reflection in the mirror. A stranger stared back, her features obscured beneath layers of grime and the harsh evidence of captivity. It was a sight I never thought I would see, but one I realized Scarlett knew well.

Beside me, Tristan rifled through the medicine cabinet, gathering supplies—bandages, antiseptic, cotton swabs, and pain relievers. "Let's get you cleaned up, but..." He hesitated, looking around the bathroom. "Should I get clothes from Scarlett and Ethan's bedroom?"

Without waiting for my response, he left the bathroom, returning a few minutes later with a bottle of water and a nightgown bundled around a few other pieces. "I felt a little weird digging through her underwear drawer," he said as he kneeled in front of where I had sat, a cheeky smile on his face, the expression cutting the tension.

I could not help but reach forward and touch his cheek, remembering the promise I'd made to myself when I thought hope was all but lost—to let him in. "I'm sure she won't mind."

As gently as he could, he tilted my chin up, his jaw tightening as he inspected a gash on my cheek. "This needs to be cleaned."

His hands were delicate as he dabbed at the wound with a cotton swab soaked in antiseptic. It stung, but I remained still, anchored in his eyes. There was such kindness and concentration on his face, that I could not look away. Each stroke of the cloth was like an eraser, slowly restoring my identity, revealing the woman who had endured, who still clung to the shards of her resolve.

"Does it hurt?" His gaze met mine, hazel green eyes searching for the truth below the surface.

"Less than before," I admitted, the pain receding under his careful ministrations. It was a curious thing, to find solace in such gentle gestures, to feel the warmth of human touch thawing the frost that had settled around my heart. "I need to take a shower. Badly."

Although we both knew I needed rest more than anything else, he did not argue, instead standing and turning on the shower, and then returning to me to help me undress. Once he lowered me down onto the bench inside the walk-in shower, he stripped off his own clothes and stepped in with me.

There was nothing sexual about how he ran the soapy washcloth across my skin, careful around the bruises, but desire still sent heat through my veins. I closed my eyes to savor it, letting the water wash away not just the physical grime, but also the remnants of fear and despair. After all the pain I had gone through, his gentle touch actually felt amazing. I was safe.

"Thank you for taking care of me." The words were not much more than a whisper, but I knew he heard them.

Ignoring the stream of water that rained down on his face, he kneeled in front of me and reached up to cup my cheek. "You don't have to thank me. I will always take care of you, Superwoman."

Just as I started to drift off, the sound of the front door banging open jolted me awake. Heavy footsteps pounded down the hallway and Tristan sat up beside me just as the door opened.

Ethan burst into the room, his eyes wild with concern. In two long strides he was at my side, dropping to his knees beside the bed.

"Cara," he breathed, his eyes roaming over me, taking in my bruises. His jaw tightened, but his fury melted as he met my gaze, replaced by tender relief. Reaching out, he brushed the hair back from my face. "Are you okay? Do you need to see a doctor?"

Without hesitation, I shook my head. "Just rest. I think I'll be okay."

More footsteps approached from the hallway, and Scarlett rushed into the room. Her dark eyes widened with worry as she took in the sight of me.

"Oh, Caroline," she said as she rushed to stand beside Ethan, her eyes widening further as she turned to look at her husband. Only then did I notice he was injured, his shoulder wrapped in a bloody piece of his shirt.

I tried to sit up in the bed, but the pain that shot through my ribs forced me back down. "What happened?"

Seeming to have just noticed he was injured as well, Ethan stood and pulled off his hoodie, revealing a gash on his arm. It was long, but did not look too deep, settling the panic in my chest some. "I'm fine. Little Red's gonna get this all taken care of."

Touching him on the cheek, Scarlett nodded in agreement. "We'll let you get to sleep, but Tristan will let us know if you need anything. I know Evie will want to see you when you wake."

Behind me, Tristan nodded. There was such a strong part of me that wanted to run down the stairs and hold my daughter, but I knew it would be a mistake. The last thing I wanted to do was wake her and scare her by seeing the state I was in. There was no doubt I would still be bruised when I woke, but I at least hoped I would be in a little better shape.

The soft click of the door closing was the last thing I heard before sleep claimed me. With Tristan beside me, I drifted into oblivion, my battered body and mind finally getting the rest they so desperately needed.

I was not sure how much time had passed before I began to stir, but I was comforted by the warm body curled around me. It had been so long since I had slept with a man, aside from the night Tristan and I spent together, but I'd missed it. One of his arms rested on my hip, the other beneath my pillow, his breath warm against my ear. His touch was soothing. For the first time since Daniel's death, I felt protected. Because even though my brother had always taken care of me, something was always missing without my husband. After everything Tristan had gone through to keep me safe, I knew he would never hurt me.

With a soft sigh, I relaxed into him, soaking up his warmth. My eyes remained closed, too heavy to open just yet, and not yet ready to face the day. Instead, I focused on the sound of his heart beating steadily beneath my ear, its rhythm strong. The rise and fall of his chest lulled me, my breathing syncing to match his. The pain in my body seemed to ebb away in his embrace. I had not realized until that moment just how much I needed this. Needed him.

A burst of bright, bubbly laughter pulled me from my slumber. I had not even intended to fall asleep again, but my body needed it, so I had. I blinked slowly, trying to clear the fog from my mind. The laughter came again, louder this time, and my heart lurched.

Evie.

My eyes flew open, searching for her, heart leaping when I saw her standing at the foot of the bed.

"Mommy, you're awake!"

My vision blurred with tears as I pulled myself to sit, ignoring my aches and pains as she flew into my arms. "Hey, nugget," I whispered hoarsely. "I missed you."

CHAPTER 31

The Survivor

Three Months Later

The sterile white delivery room seemed to blur and swirl as another contraction sent pain cascading through my body, a tidal force that left me gasping, clutching desperately at the steel railings of the hospital bed. My world had narrowed down to the crushing pressure in my belly, causing me to grit my teeth and scream. The pain was a living thing, an entity that gripped me from the inside out, demanding everything from me. At the end of it, however, we would have our daughter, and that was worth it all.

"You're doing great, Little Red. Just breathe." Ethan's voice was an anchor in the midst of the storm raging through me, his calloused hand giving me something better to squeeze. "Almost there," he whispered, his light blue eyes locking onto mine. "And then she'll be here."

Not looking away from him, I clenched my jaw so hard it hurt, crying out through my clenched teeth. Still, his presence was unwavering, every squeeze of his hand a lifeline back to him, to us, to the life we had forged from the ashes of our haunted pasts. It calmed me.

"Focus on me, love." Hand sliding up my cheek, he brushed a strand of hair from my sweat-drenched forehead and kissed me. "I'm right here. We're in this together, just like always."

I drew in a shuddering breath, trying to steady the tremors that racked up my body, but as soon as I calmed, another contraction ripped through me.

"It's time to push, Scarlett." Getting into position, the doctor placed her hand on my belly. "With your next contraction, I need you to bare down and push as hard as you can."

And then I pushed, not just against the physical barrier, but against the remnants of the woman I used to be—the one who believed she was unworthy of love, undeserving of happiness. With Ethan's hand in mine, encouraging me with his words, I pressed my chin to my chest and pushed.

My daughter's first cry pierced the sterile air, the sweet sound heralding the end of one journey and the beginning of another. As a storm of emotions more powerful than anything I had ever experienced flooded through me, leaving me a trembling, sobbing mess, a tiny wriggling baby with a head of thick black hair was placed on my chest.

Ethan leaned closer, his eyes glassy as his fingers trailed across her cheek—so unbelievably gentle for such a lethal man. "She's perfect, Little Red. Just like you."

"Congratulations, Mom and Dad," the doctor said with a smile. "She's beautiful."

"Hello, my little Adelaide," I whispered, touching her tiny fingers, making sure there were ten.

The nurse handed Ethan a pair of surgical scissors. "Whenever you're ready, Dad, you can cut the cord."

For a man who had spent most of his life with a heart made of steel, his hands trembled as he reached down and cut the cord connecting our baby to me. There was so much more tenderness inside him than even he was willing to admit, but it was why I loved him as much as I did.

Tears blurred my vision as I held our daughter in my arms, with Ethan's cheek a mere breath away. It was not from pain or sorrow, but from an overwhelming sense of fulfillment. I had carried and nurtured this precious life within me, and now she was here, the physical embodiment of everything Ethan and I had forged together. The ghosts of my past, once shackled to my every step, seemed to dissipate in the reflection of her dark and inquisitive eyes. The rest did not matter anymore. With the enemies gone or locked away, we could finally move on with our lives as a family, no longer overshadowed by darkness. With Adelaide, in came the light.

CHAPTER 32

The Phoenix

Three Months Later

A delicious heat unfurled within me, spreading through my veins as Tristan's fingers danced across my skin, caressing my curves. His lips trailed kisses down the column of my neck, chasing that fire with shivers. Being with Tristan made the darkness fade, chasing away the shadows that lingered in my soul. Ever since we had been together, the wounds of my soul had begun to heal, the sharp edges softening until I could finally breathe again.

"You're so beautiful, Superwoman," he whispered, his breath fanning against my collarbone. I tangled my fingers in his hair and pulled his lips back to mine, slipping my tongue inside to taste him.

When I pulled away, looking into his hazel green eyes, I was breathless. "You're not so bad yourself, Super Spy." The side of his lips lifted in a grin that made my heart flip. He was so fucking sexy, in that 'just rolled out of bed, hot even though he doesn't try and doesn't know it,' kind of way. "And you're a smug bastard about it too."

He chuckled, knowing it was true. Placing one more lingering kiss on my lips, he slid down my body, kissing his way down my breasts and my stomach.

I whimpered as he settled between my thighs, nudging them wider apart, and he wasted no time giving me what I needed. He never did.

Tongue delving between my folds, he lapped at my clit with slow, languid strokes, his massive hand gripping my thigh to hold it open. Sparks of pleasure ignited within me, burning hotter and brighter with each pass of his skilled mouth. We did not discuss our past sexual endeavors, but it was clear by how he touched me that he'd had a good teacher at some point in time, or perhaps he was just a natural. It did not matter, as long as I was the only woman he touched for the rest of his life. It had only been seven months, but he was endgame for me. His ability to give me multiple mind-blowing orgasms in one night only made me want to keep him more.

Fingers curling into his hair, I urged him closer, my back rolling of its own accord. He groaned, the vibrations only sending more sensations through my core. The way he worshipped my body was truly something to be admired. It was as though he enjoyed it more than I did, which I highly doubted, but would never argue.

"Fuck, Tris—" My words broke into a gasp when his long fingers slid inside me, one followed by another, stroking that upper wall that made my toes curl. Ecstasy spiraled deep in my belly, twisting so tight that I thought I might burst. I rolled my hips, chasing the bliss I knew was coming.

With one hand still tangled in his hair, the other gripped the blanket, bringing it to my face as the sounds coming out of my mouth became louder—more desperate. It was the middle of the night, and my daughter was asleep, but the walls were not thick enough for how this felt, and I could not hold it in. The moment the fabric covered my mouth, I fractured.

White-hot ecstasy flooded my veins, my body arching off the bed as wave after wave of pleasure crashed over me. I cried out into the cotton, my eyes watering from the intensity—from the tendrils of electricity that branched out across my body like lightning.

When the aftershocks eased, leaving me limp but not nearly done, he kissed his way up my body, wiping his mouth with the back of his hand, where the evidence of my orgasm still glistened on his lips. Still panting heavily, I pulled his mouth to mine, tasting myself on his tongue.

"I need you," I said against his lips, reaching down to grip his length with my hand. Tristan shifted, nudging my entrance with the broad head of his cock.

Lifting my hips, I welcomed him in, loving how his size always filled me to the point of near pain, but a pain that made me beg for more. I dug my nails into his back, and he hissed, quickening his pace.

"Come for me," he whispered against my lips, but I did not need him to tell me. I was already halfway there.

His strokes were powerful, and I met every one with one of my own. Sex between us was primal, the need I felt for him all consuming.

Just when I thought he could not possibly get any deeper, he gripped my hip and angled it up as he pulled out of our kiss to hook my leg over his shoulder. I clung to him, drowning in pleasure as his hips thrusted into mine, bringing my orgasm back to the surface. My eyes rolled back in my head as I moaned into the blanket, grasping his thigh for purchase, digging my nails in.

Growling my name, or some semblance of it, his gaze locked with mine, and I knew he was close. His thrusts became erratic, but my orgasm only grew stronger, the squeeze of my pussy around him bringing tears to my eyes. I pulled him back against me as his climax shuddered his movements, swallowing his moans with my mouth.

As we collapsed on the bed, sweating and sated, I smiled up at him, so many words on my tongue that I wanted to say. I had such gratitude for this man who had fought his way into my heart, for being my strength when I felt like I had none left, for seeing the real me behind the masks I wore and cherishing each part.

"Thank you." My voice was soft, not because I did not want him to hear, but because he was close enough to hear even my heartbeat. "For loving me."

He smiled, brushing my hair away from my face and pressing a lingering kiss on my lips. "Thank you for giving me the chance."

Evie squealed as we entered the gates of Disney World, her eyes widening at the sight of the castle in the distance. Although her hair was still no more than a pixie cut, a sparkly crown adorned her head, and she had on a fluffy yellow dress over her T-shirt and tights. With a smile that stretched from ear to ear, her eyes shimmered, reflecting the wonder of a child who had faced down darkness and emerged into the light. My heart swelled, heavy with a love so profound it bordered on pain. Evie's battle with Leukemia had been a tempest that threatened to swallow us whole for years, but there she was, the embodiment of resilience, ready to have the time of her life, and we were all there to experience it with her.

Squeezing Tristan's hand, I had to blink back tears at seeing the pure joy on my daughter's face. With my other hand in Evie's, we allowed her to lead the way. Scarlett and Ethan walked right beside us, baby Adelaide asleep in the carrier strapped to my brother's chest. It had been a difficult year, but we had made it through the darkness together as a family. This trip was a celebration of Evie's one year anniversary of being in remission, a wish granted as we stepped forward into our future together, leaving the darkness of our pasts behind.

"Look, Mommy!" Evie said, her excited voice pulling me from my reverie. "We're almost there!"

Tristan smiled down at her, flicking her button nose. "Are you excited, Captain?"

With a fit of giggles, she swatted him away. "Super excited!" Excitement bubbling over, she jumped up and down. "Mommy, do you think fairy tales are real?"

"Sometimes," I said, unfettered joy making my heart swell. "I think life gives us our own kind of fairy tale."

"Like ours?" she asked, her gaze scanning the five of us standing before her, sharing in her sunshine.

I nodded, reaching out to touch her cheek. "Exactly like ours."

As we made our way toward the iconic landmark, weaving through the clusters of excited families, I could not help but think about how far our little family had come—how much we had all changed, individually and as a team. Just like Scarlett and Ethan, Tristan and I had come together against all odds, and with Evie in tow, my ex-assassin brother, bookstore owning sister-in-law with a painful past, and a brand new baby niece, we had somehow created our own version of a happily ever after...if you believed in that sort of thing.

THE END

Enjoyed
Keeping Caroline?

Thank you so much for reading Keeping Caroline!
I hope that you enjoyed how I tied up this duet! If
you enjoyed Keeping Caroline, please leave a
review! It truly helps to get my books in the
hands of more readers!
https://www.amazon.com/dp/B0CPWJDZ6N

Sign up for C. A. Varian's newsletter to receive
current updates on her new and upcoming
releases, sales, and giveaways:
https://sendfox.com/cavarian

You can also find all stories, books, and social
media pages and follow her here:
https://linktr.ee/cavarian
https://cavarian.com/

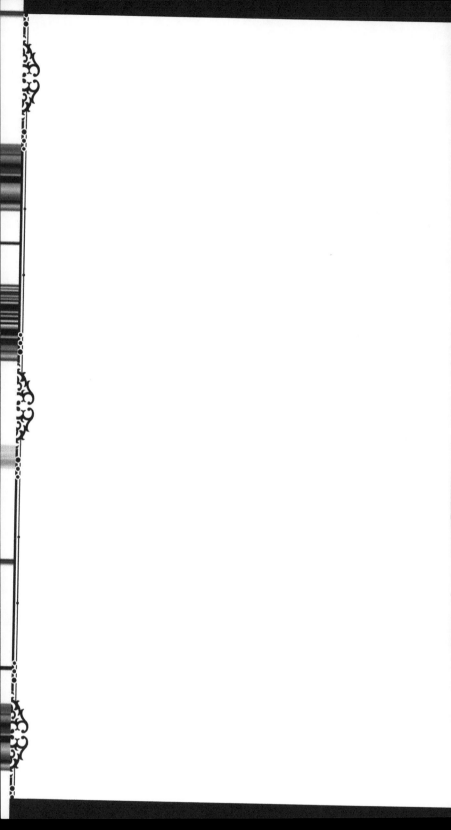

Acknowledgements

I want to thank my editor, Megan, of Willow Oak Author services, for putting up with my crazy editing schedule. (At least I keep the work coming).

I would also like to thank Kristen from Wiski Publishing, LLC., for proofreading and a second edit.

I would like to thank Leigh Cadiente of Leigh Cover Designs for this gorgeous cover.

Thank you to Breezy Jones for the amazing art and for being my BFF.

Thank you to my Personal Assistants: Jasmine, Jessica, Jordan, and Aly. I don't know what I would do without you guys.

Thank you to Timothy Higgins from Swampy Sloth Studios for all the gorgeous art created for this series.

Thank you so much to my phenomenal Street Team, Mikela Jones, Laura Farrell, Sierra Crawford, Amber Gamble, Jule Hayes, LeeRenee Musgjerd, Pyro Ember, Tasha Melton, Samantha Gentry, Chelsea Savage, Halley Peagler, Jeanann Leary, Illisa Lea, Michele Vaughan, Jessica Spain, Debbie Webb, Autumn Gresser-Chambers, Nichole Crawley, Yvonne Aguilera, Lauren Landry, Karina Serrano, Kerrie Porter, Natali Garcia, Molly Mazure, Destiny Del Palacio, Yesenia Rosado, Kass Scholes, Cortni Jo Werkema, Kira Diduck, and a few others! You guys are so good to me!

My final thank you is to my family, friends, and most of all, my readers.

Thank you for your support!

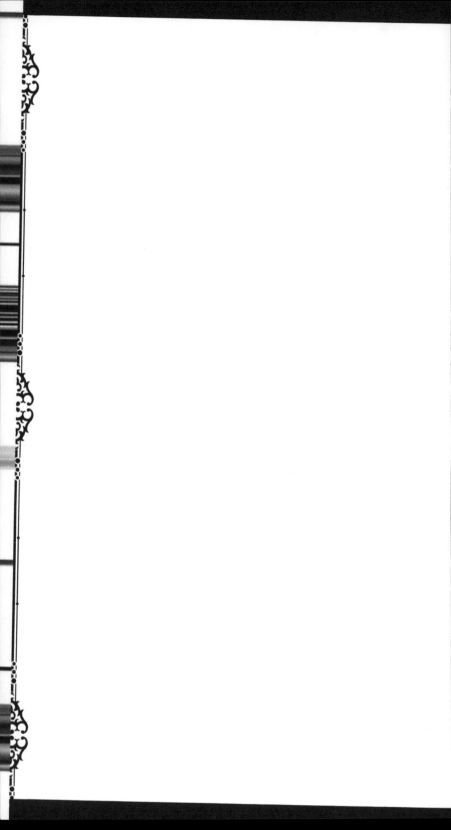

Also By

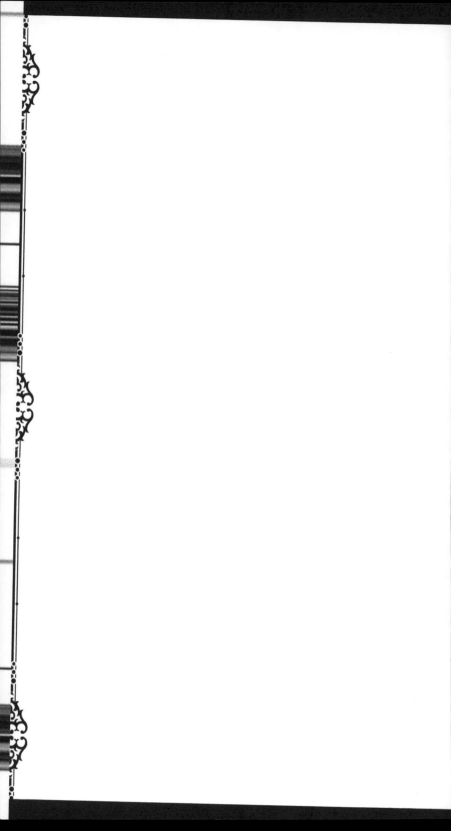

About the Author

Raised in a small town in the heart of Louisiana's Cajun Country, C. A. Varian spent most of her childhood fishing, crabbing, and getting sunburnt at the beach. Her love of reading began very young, and she would often participate in school reading challenges.

Graduating with the first of her college degrees as a mother of two in her late twenties, she became a public-school teacher, teaching for twelve years, both social studies and special education. As of the release of this book, she was finally able to resign from teaching to write full time!

Writing became a passion project, and she put out her first novel in 2021. She has continued to publish new novels every few months since then, not slowing down for even a minute.

Married to a retired military officer, she spent many years moving around for his career, but they currently live in central Alabama, along with her youngest daughter, Arianna. Her oldest daughter, Brianna, is enjoying her happily ever after with her new husband and several pups. C.A. Varian has two Shih Tzus that she considers her children. Boy, Charlie, and girl, Luna, are their mommy's shadows. She also has three cats named Ramses, Simba, and Cookie.

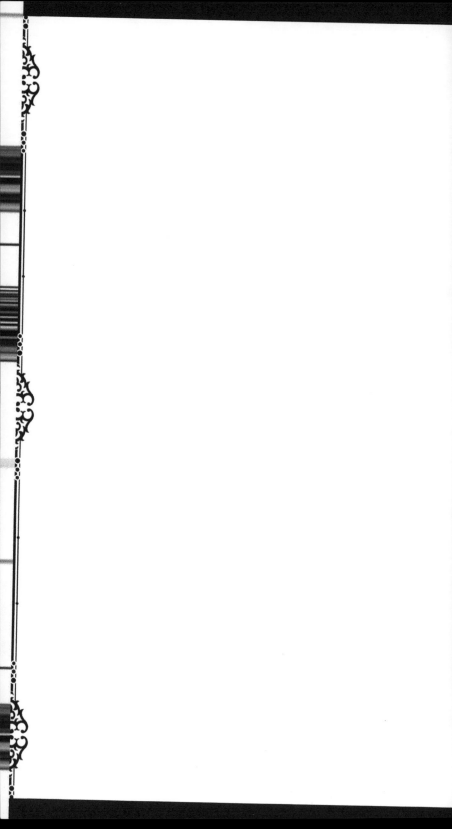

9 781961 23838